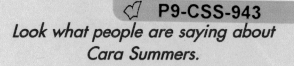
*Look what people are saying about
Cara Summers.*

"Cara Summers knows how to write fun yet
passionate plots that readers will never forget."
—*Romance Junkies*

"I can't wait to read more by Cara Summers."
—*The Best Reviews*

"Ms. Summers is a compelling storyteller with a
gift for emotional and dramatic prose."
—*Rendezvous*

"With exquisite flair, Ms. Summers thrills us
with her fresh, exciting voice as well as rich
characterization and spicy adventure."
—*RT Book Reviews*

"A writer of incredible talent with a gift for
emotional stories laced with humor and passion."
—*Rendezvous*

"A great mystery. The excitement and romance
never end. Top Pick."
—*RT Book Reviews* on *Christmas Male*

# Blaze

Dear Reader,

When the Brightman sisters open Haworth House, a small hotel on an island off the coast of Maine, they get more than they bargained for—including Hattie Haworth, a resident ghost who can transform their most secret fantasies into reality....

And she's going to do it again for a few lucky couples attending a special singles' weekend.

As the youngest of three sisters, workaholic five-star chef Reese Brightman has always followed the path of least resistance. But no more. Now she's going to take charge of her life, starting with fulfilling the secret fantasy she drew out of Hattie's hat box.

Not only is lounge singer Brie Sullivan the star witness in the murder trial of a mob boss, but her first bodyguard has been shot. When she meets her new protector, former CIA agent Cody Marsh, the thrill of having him watch over her, day and night, definitely takes her mind off her problems.

I've had so much fun writing this ENCOUNTERS/ FORBIDDEN FANTASY book. It's allowed me to bring to a conclusion all the stories that I began in my May and June Blaze books, *Led into Temptation* and *Taken Beyond Temptation*. I hope you enjoy these stories as much as I did.

Love and laughter always,

Cara Summers

# Cara Summers

## TWICE THE TEMPTATION

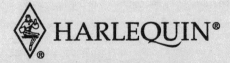

HARLEQUIN®

TORONTO • NEW YORK • LONDON
AMSTERDAM • PARIS • SYDNEY • HAMBURG
STOCKHOLM • ATHENS • TOKYO • MILAN • MADRID
PRAGUE • WARSAW • BUDAPEST • AUCKLAND

Recycling programs
for this product may
not exist in your area.

ISBN-13: 978-0-373-79559-8

TWICE THE TEMPTATION

Copyright © 2010 by Carolyn Hanlon.

www.eHarlequin.com

**Printed in U.S.A.**

## ABOUT THE AUTHOR

Was Cara Summers born with the dream of becoming a published romance novelist? No. But now that she is, she still feels her dream has come true. She loves writing for the Blaze line because it allows her to create strong, determined women and seriously sexy men who will risk everything to achieve *their* dreams. Cara has written more than thirty books for Harlequin, and when she isn't working on new stories, she teaches in the Writing Program at Syracuse University and at a community college near her home.

## Books by Cara Summers

### HARLEQUIN BLAZE

To my brother Andy who reads all of
my books and thinks I'm a better writer than
"Billy" Shakespeare! You are definitely my
biggest fan. And thanks for posing for all of my
covers, too! I love you!

# *Prologue*

MAKING A SALES PITCH to a ghost wasn't something they'd covered in the MBA program at Harvard's Business School. No, indeedy, thought Avery Cooper as he stepped into the tower room where the spirit of legendary film star Hattie Haworth had resided for some forty-five years.

Avery straightened his tie and took a deep breath. He'd been managing the Haworth House hotel for the Brightman sisters well over a year now, and he'd known right from the get-go that the original owner haunted the place. The story was that she'd fled to Belle Island to build her new home when both her marriage and her career had tanked in Hollywood.

She'd appeared to all three of the sisters right in this very room. Jillian Brightman, his best friend and ex-college roommate, had included that piece of information when she'd hired him to manage the hotel.

Avery doubted that a dozen ghosts could have deterred him from accepting her job offer. Not once Jillian had explained what she and her sisters, Naomi and Reese, had in mind. And now, the picture she'd painted for him—a small exclusive hotel on an island off the coast of Maine—had become a reality.

He let his gaze sweep the tower room. Late afternoon sunlight slanted through a circle of windows, and the muted sound of the sea could be heard crashing on the rocks below. During the renovation, the tower room had been turned into an office/sitting room where each of the sisters worked when they were in residence. But fifty-five years ago, this was where Hattie Haworth and her lover, a man from the village, had shared their love and lived out their fantasies for nearly a year.

*You're stalling.* Avery frowned. What in the world was wrong with him? In his line of work, he was never at a loss for words. And Hattie Haworth had already proven that she loved the sisters as much as he did. Not only had she played a role in saving both Naomi's and Jillian's lives but she'd brought them each together with their true loves by satisfying their most secret fantasies.

And the fantasies were what he needed to talk to Hattie about. Avery strode forward until he stood in front of the gilt-framed, beveled mirror. Peering into it, all he could see was his own reflection—a tall, broad-shouldered, dark-skinned man in his late twenties. His grandmother would have approved of the clothes—a suit, tie and shirt in varying shades of gray. Grandma Cooper had always told him that it was important to dress well.

He could only hope that Hattie shared that opinion. But so far, he saw no sign of that in the glass. All three of the sisters claimed to have glimpsed Hattie Haworth's image in the mirror. Naomi and Jillian had also claimed to have carried on one-sided conversations with her.

*Shit.* He fingered his tie again. He hadn't been this

nervous when he'd defended his Masters thesis at Harvard.

"Hattie, I'm Avery Cooper. You may have seen me around."

*Duh. Get to the point.* "I came to talk to you about an idea I have. It concerns your fantasy box and Reese."

Avery blinked, then narrowed his eyes. Was that the tiniest flash of light he'd seen in the mirror?

"Jillian told me all about how she found your secret room and the hat box with the fantasies in it, how she and her sisters each chose an envelope out of it on the night they bought Haworth House."

He paused, but saw nothing in the mirror. Had he imagined it?

"Okay, old news. But I want you to know that I think the world of the two men Naomi and Jillian have hooked up with as a result of those fantasies. Dane and Ian Mac-Farland are the best." In his opinion, the two men were perfect matches for Naomi and Jillian. Now, if Hattie could just work the same magic for Reese...

This time he was sure he saw a shimmer of light. Just for an instant. But it was enough to make his heart skip a beat.

*Okay, you've got her attention. Now all you have to do is sell it.*

"I have this idea. Reese is a bang-up chef. The whole menu here at the hotel is hers. And she designed the kitchen. She's so good that the pilot she filmed for a syndicated cooking show in L.A. has just sold thirteen episodes."

*Get to the point.* "But she hasn't been back to visit the hotel in a while. She's moved all her stuff in, but she hasn't really made the place her home. Reese claims she's too busy. But even now, when she's on a break from filming her new TV series, she's holed up in L.A."

Avery stepped closer to the mirror. "I'm wondering if she's worried about that parchment envelope she drew out of your fantasy box. You know, you're two for two in the fantasy-fulfillment department. If I'd drawn one out, I might be a little nervous, too."

When he paused to take a breath, Avery was almost sure he heard a sound. Laughter?

Narrowing his eyes, he raised both hands, palms outward. "Don't get any ideas. I'm okay in the fantasy department. My partner and I are very happy."

Nothing.

*When in doubt, forge ahead.* "The thing is, I'd like to see Reese as happy as her sisters." He cleared his throat. "And she's not. What I think she needs is a good nudge. And you're the best nudger I know. So I came up with the idea of offering a Singles Weekend here at the hotel, one that would include events—beach picnics and other activities like hiking and sailing—so that singles with similar interests can hook up with each other. I did some fast talking and convinced Reese she needed to be here for it. Her sisters and their fiancés are all traveling and I told her one of the owners had to be around." He waved a hand. "Yada, yada, yada. I've even persuaded her to do a little hands-on cooking demo on Sunday afternoon for the foodies."

Avery stopped and drew in a deep breath.

When he paused this time, there were no lights, no laughs. He *hoped* he was good at selling ideas. But he hadn't mentioned the kicker yet.

"Once she's here, I figure it will be up to you to handle the rest, the way you did for her sisters." He drew in a breath and let it out. "But here's the part I thought I ought to talk to you about."

Nothing.

"I want to use the fantasies in your box as an added marketing draw. We'll have a mixer party on the first night and allow those singles interested to draw out one of the parchment envelopes. We might not get any takers, considering that only the locals know about your fantasy box. The sisters have kept it pretty quiet. But when I was thinking about how to get Reese here for a few days so that you could deal with her fantasy, I thought, why not offer the opportunity to someone else? And then…" Avery waved a hand. "What will happen, will happen."

Any minute now he was going to break out into a chorus of "Que sera, sera" from that old Doris Day film.

For a moment the air around him stilled. And in the reflection in the mirror, he saw a panel in the wall behind him slide open.

The secret room.

He'd heard Naomi and Jillian both speak of it, but he'd never seen it. Turning, he strode to it, and sure enough, there on the floor was a linen-covered hat box. Lifting it, he carried it with him to face the mirror again.

On the cover he read the words *Fantasy Box: Choose carefully. The one you draw out will come true.*

Though the sisters had all spoken about the warning, seeing the words for the first time sent a little shiver up Avery's spine.

He shifted his gaze to the mirror. "This isn't for the faint of heart. But I'm going to assume I have your approval."

For a moment, he could have sworn that the sound

of the ocean grew louder. Then he saw two images take form in the mirror—a woman in a long white dress with reddish gold curls falling to her shoulders and a tall man with fair hair standing with her, their hands joined.

Both of them were smiling.

Even after the images faded, Avery stared into the glass for a long time.

# PLAYING WITH REESE

# 1

*Thursday morning—the day before Singles Weekend*

THIS IS THE DAY I'M TAKING *charge of my life*.

At least that was the plan, Reese reminded herself as she got out of the van in the driveway of Haworth House. Shading her eyes, she glanced up at the tower, the place she and her sisters now called home. A home she'd moved all her belongings into and then allowed a ghost to scare her away from.

Not that she was afraid of Hattie Haworth herself. After all, she owed the silent film star big time for saving the lives of her two sisters and bringing them each together with a man they'd fallen in love with—Dane and Ian MacFarland. It was the fantasy she'd drawn out of Hattie's fantasy box, along with Hattie's matchmaking skill that had kept her from really settling in at Haworth House.

Well, that was going to stop. She was twenty-four years old, and Reese Brightman's M.O. was about to change. No more running away. No more letting the people who cared about her push roadblocks out of her path.

That had been the history of her life so far. She'd been a baby, her sisters a few years older when they'd lost their mother, and their father had left them in the care of the nuns at a Catholic boarding school in the south of France. Six months later, when he, too, had died, the good sisters had kept them and raised them. All of her life, there'd been people taking care of her, making her life run smoothly, eliminating obstacles when they appeared in her path.

From now on, she was going to deal with her own problems. And first on her list was taking care of the silly fantasy she'd drawn out of Hattie's fantasy box. Avery's phone call inviting her to help launch the hotel's first Singles Weekend was just the nudge she'd needed.

For starters, it allowed her to take a reprieve from her problems in L.A. Just thinking about the two anonymous notes she'd received during the last two weeks had fear bubbling up again. Ruthlessly, she shoved it down. She wasn't a wimp. She might have ignored the notes if they both hadn't been accompanied by a single black rose. It was the roses that gave her the willies.

And then there was the finicky producer of her TV cooking show, Mr. Can't-Make-Up-His-Mind Mac Davies, who after shooting three different pilots, was still waffling about the setting for the thirteen episodes they'd sold. According to her agent, Davies' staff was scouting out locations and filming was on hold until he found the perfect one. And she should be patient.

Usually, she was. Usually, she was quite willing to let events run their course. But this TV show was the biggest thing that had ever happened to her so far. And it frustrated her that Mac Davies hadn't once asked for her input. Both times she'd tried to make a personal appointment with him, he'd refused to see her. And she'd let him get away with that. Shading her eyes, she frowned up at the tower. That was the old Reese Brightman.

"Your bag, Ms. Brightman."

Reese shifted her gaze to the young man who'd driven her from the ferry.

"Would you like me to carry it into the lobby for you?"

"No thanks, Larry." Noticing the surprised look on his face, Reese smiled as she took her duffel. "I can manage." She wasn't quite ready to go inside and talk to Avery yet.

She needed to gather her thoughts and have a little chat with Hattie. As soon as the van drove away, she strode down the driveway, and after a quick look around to make sure the driveway was deserted, she pulled a parchment envelope out of her pocket, then narrowed her eyes once more on the semi-circle of windows in the tower. "Because of you, I've been avoiding this place like the plague."

As soon as the words were out, a ribbon of guilt wound its way up her spine. "Okay, okay, maybe it's not all your fault." Her schedule had been very busy—finishing her first book tour and then filming those three pilots for the hard-to-please Mac Davies.

"Part of the blame can be laid at the door of my boy-genius producer, Mac Davies. In the first pilot, I was a French pastry chef and the whole set was pink. Yuck! Then he changed his mind and turned me into a ditsy housewife giving everyday dishes a gourmet flair. Double yuck!"

Reese blinked. Had it been her imagination or had

she seen a figure at one of the windows? Hattie had been pretty familiar with the L.A. scene some sixty-plus years ago. Maybe it hadn't changed all that much. Encouraged, she continued, "I've never met this producer, but my agent urged me to be patient. Evidently, Mac Davies is the guy the networks go to when they want to raise ratings. Every show he's produced so far has been an Emmy-winning hit."

Reese frowned and waved the parchment envelope. "And that is *not* what I want to talk to you about. It's this ridiculous fantasy."

And it was ridiculous. But telling herself that hadn't stopped a tingle of anticipation every time she thought about it.

Drawing a deep breath, she pulled the parchment out of the envelope and read the words again. *You will explore all the sensual delights of having your own boy toy.*

*Boy toy.*

Just looking at the words had her skin heating, her breath catching. The nerves in her stomach danced their way into a regular highland fling.

Tucking the parchment back into the envelope, she shot an accusing glance at the tower. "Having a boy toy has never been my fantasy."

At least it never had been before.

Frustrated, she began to pace back and forth in the driveway. "Naomi and Jillian both drew out fantasies that they'd entertained before. So I figured you'd made a mistake with me." She'd never had the time nor the inclination to…what? Play with a boy toy?

"Fantasies," she muttered. Maybe that was the way Hattie and her lover had chosen to spend their time. And that was fine. Considering what had come to light about Hattie's affair with Samuel Jenkins and its tragic ending, she didn't begrudge them any of the short time they'd had together. But she had better things to do.

"I simply don't have time for men. Been there. Done that." For the first time in years, Reese found herself remembering the man she'd met when she'd first entered Le Cordon Bleu. Charlie Dutoit had been one of her classmates. He'd been handsome and charming, and she'd been young. It had been April in Paris and she'd fallen hard. When he'd dumped her two weeks before graduation, she'd run back to the boarding school and very nearly given up on her dream of becoming a world-class chef.

That had been five years ago, and so much had happened since then. Reese stopped short and whirled to face the tower windows again. She hadn't thought of Charlie in years. So why was she thinking about him now?

She glanced down at the envelope she still held in her hand. Was she worried about more than the fantasy?

Narrowing her eyes, she shifted her gaze to the windows again. "Maybe it *is* more than the fantasy I'm nervous about. At first I might have stayed away because I thought you made a mistake. But I've seen what you've done with my sisters. You made a lot more than just their fantasies come true. Dane MacFarland is perfect for Naomi, and Ian is exactly right for Jillian."

Was that the real source of her skittish nerves?

She fisted her hands on her hips. "I'm not interested in having a man in my life right now."

*But a boy toy...?*

Even as the words formed in her mind, Reese was sure she saw two figures standing in one of the windows. Then they faded. But the words in her mind lingered.

*A boy toy…*

Reese glanced down at the envelope. Was it possible that she was still letting a betrayal that had happened five years ago affect her life? Was it possible that Charlie Dutoit still had her doubting her own judgment when it came to men?

Well, *not* anymore.

She shifted her gaze to the front door of the hotel. She held in her hand an, as yet, unfulfilled fantasy and she was going to a Singles Weekend—for better or worse.

When she glanced back up at the tower, she saw nothing but the windows. "I know you're there, Hattie, and here's the deal. I'm not letting you or anyone else push me into something I'm not ready for. I've come to help Avery launch the hotel's first Singles Weekend. If I decide to enjoy a boy toy, it will be my decision."

*This* is *the day I'm taking charge of my life.*

Reese strode to the hotel steps and took them two at a time. She had to let Avery know she was here a day early. Then they could talk about what he wanted her to contribute to his big Singles Weekend. He'd mentioned a sunset cookout on the beach, a volleyball tournament, as well as hiking and sailing day trips. And she had to firm up the cooking demo he wanted her to do on Sunday. Then, of course, there would be the big singles mixer tomorrow night that would include a chance to draw a fantasy from Hattie's box.

The door of the hotel swung open. As she dashed through it, she glanced down to see she was still holding the envelope with the fantasy she'd drawn gripped tightly in her hand. And in that moment of inattention, she ran full tilt into a solid wall of muscle and man.

Her breath whooshed out, her duffel and the envelope both went flying as she shot backward onto her butt.

For a moment, all she could do was stare at the long, denim-clad legs in front of her.

Then before she could blink or even draw in a breath, two strong hands gripped her wrists and pulled her to her feet. She was tall, but she had to glance up to meet his eyes. They were so blue, they seemed to burn right through her.

Her pulse raced frantically against the pressure of those long, lean fingers. But it wasn't just awareness that moved through her. There was a ripple of something else. Recognition?

"Sorry. Are you all right?"

Reese thought she managed a nod. But several things were distracting her. He was so big, his shoulders so broad. The hands that had moved to her upper arms were large and very male. She was very aware of the heat of them against her bare skin.

"You're sure you're all right?"

She couldn't manage more than another nod because she couldn't seem to breathe yet, and her knees felt weak. Those incredibly blue eyes held her captive, but she still noticed the handsome face with the warrior cheekbones, the strong chin. It was a wonder that the modeling industry hadn't snapped him up and made him a media star. His dark hair looked mussed as if someone had just run her hands through it.

*Her hands?* Even as her palms tingled, Reese felt heat rush through her—the same kind she'd felt each time she'd let herself think about the boy toy fantasy.

*Her fantasy! Where was it?*

"My…things."

She pulled away, dropped to her knees and glanced frantically around for the envelope. Spotting it just behind him, she reached for it at the same time he did.

When she jerked it away, she ended up with the envelope and he the message.

Panic and embarrassment raced for first place when she saw him glance down at it.

What would he think? What could she say? Her first impulse was to get to her feet and run. But she was through with that.

"Here."

She didn't have the courage to meet his eyes when she took it from his outstretched hand. But she hadn't run. "Thanks," she managed as she stuffed it into the envelope and crammed both into her pocket. Then she scrambled to her feet.

"You're sure you're all right?" he asked as he handed her the duffel.

*No.*

She drew in the first full breath she'd taken since she'd run into him. "Absolutely." One way or another, she was going to face head-on what life dealt her. Lifting her chin, she met his eyes.

Relief flooded her when she read nothing in his gaze. No laughter, no questions, not even curiosity. Perhaps he hadn't read the words, after all.

*It's not disappointment I'm feeling. Really.*

"Reese, my darling girl."

Even more relief flooded through her when she saw Avery hurrying toward her. He'd called her *my darling girl* from the first moment that her sister Jillian had introduced him to her, and the endearment never failed to warm her.

When she ran into his arms, he scooped her up and swung her around. "You're early."

"Only a day."

"Well, you've made mine! I can definitely use your

help. I just booked the last room to one of Ian MacFarland's old buddies from his CIA days, Cody Marsh. You remember him?"

"Of course. He helped Ian save Jillian's life. And he has a gift for sensing and often seeing ghosts, right?"

"That's him." Avery grinned at her. "He's been anxious to get back here ever since he saw Hattie's lover on the cliff walk. I think the Singles Weekend will provide him with a few more sightings."

Reese's stomach clenched. "You're expecting Hattie to play an active role, then?"

"It's *her* fantasy box."

Perhaps Hattie had already gotten involved. As she let Avery draw her farther into the lobby, Reese couldn't prevent herself from taking a quick look over her shoulder.

Blue Eyes was just walking out the lobby door. As she ran her gaze over the broad shoulders, the narrow waist and those long, long legs, she felt a pull. For an instant, she was so tempted to run after him that she nearly pulled her arm out of Avery's grip.

Then he was gone. And this time, she couldn't deny it was disappointment she was feeling.

"Reese? Is something wrong?"

She glanced up at Avery and managed a smile. "No."

Holding her at arm's length, he let his eyes roam over her. "It amazes me that you can always manage to look elegant in jeans and a T-shirt."

Reese made a snorting sound. "Don't you start in on me. Now that Jillian has influenced Naomi into dressing more stylishly, they're both telling me I need a new wardrobe. And I don't. Why bother when I practically live in a chef's coat, anyway?"

"Because you're a bit of a workaholic."

Reese's eyebrows shot up. "And you're not?"

"The difference is I know how to play. And you need to do more of it. Molly Pepperman, who runs the boutique in the village, is going to be a guest this weekend. I asked her to talk to you about clothes designed more for play. Just a few special pieces."

"Molly's coming as a guest?"

"Yes, she is. She's talked her grandmother into coming and taking over the store for the weekend. Miss Emmy Lou Pritchard, our local librarian, is also a guest. She and Molly each want a shot at making a secret fantasy come true."

Nerves danced in Reese's stomach as the image of Blue Eyes filled her mind. If anyone fit the description of a boy toy, he did.

"People are coming from all over for this Singles Weekend. In fact, there's even someone who's come a long way to see you. He claims he's an old friend."

"Who?"

"Can't spoil the surprise," Avery said as he drew her along through the archway into a courtyard that served as extra dining space when the weather permitted.

"There he is over by that pillar."

When Reese glanced over to where Avery was pointing, she saw a tall man with his back toward her and a shorter woman in a wide-brimmed straw hat. "Who is it?"

"Charles Dutoit," Avery said. "He claims the two of you were very tight five years ago in Paris."

Charlie? Nerves tightened in her stomach. Could it be? But as the man began to turn toward them, recognition trickled in. He wore his hair close cropped to his head now. When she'd known him in Paris, he'd had to tie it back from his face with a leather thong. His face was leaner, too, the angles more pronounced, his jaw more firm. Her eyes dropped to his mouth. He had the same charming smile he'd had five years ago when she'd fallen in love with him.

She wanted to hold back when Avery drew her forward. But she made herself put one foot in front of the other and murmured in a low voice, "Of all the gin joints in all the world—"

Avery's crack of laughter turned heads and gave Reese the courage to meet Charlie's eyes as he moved to take both of her hands.

"Reese. You're as lovely as ever."

Relief streamed through her. It was Charlie all right. There was that same intent look in his eyes that had captivated her in Paris, but whatever spell he'd had over her when she'd been nineteen had been broken. She felt nothing but a vague curiosity as she returned his smile.

He kissed the fingers of one hand, then the other. It was a practiced gesture that had made her heart flutter in Paris. No flutters today.

"Charlie, it's good to see you," she said. And she meant it.

"He goes by Charles now. To match his restaurant and cookware brands, Avec Charles."

Reese shifted her attention to the deep-voiced woman at Charlie's side. She couldn't see much of her because of the wide brimmed hat and sunglasses. When the woman held out her hand, Reese pulled hers out of Charlie's to grasp it.

"I'm Annie Thornway, Charles's publicist."

"Nice to meet you." Then Reese turned back to

Charlie. "Congratulations. Your own restaurant and a cookware brand. That's amazing."

"And I'm thinking of expanding."

"He's checking out locations for a restaurant in the North East," the woman said. "Someone we ran into raved about your cooking and—"

Charlie waved a hand to silence her. "I don't want to talk about business. I wanted to see you, Reese. I need to talk to you. I made a huge mistake in Paris, and I want to do what I can to make amends. Join me for coffee. We can catch up with each other."

Reese managed to step on Avery's foot before he could agree. "Later, perhaps. Avery and I have business to discuss. We have a big weekend coming up."

"A Singles Weekend that will fulfill your secret fantasies," Annie Thornway said. "Charles picked up one of the brochures. You even have a matchmaking ghost on the premises."

Reese had time to catch the annoyance in her tone before Charlie said, "Reese, can't you see it's fate that we've met here in this time and this place? Please, join me for dinner."

Fate? Reese felt a ripple of something close to panic before she forced herself to get a grip. She was not going to let herself be pushed into anything. "I can't, Charlie. Avery and I are working tonight."

"Since you're here, you might consider getting in on the fun," Avery said smoothly to the couple. "We're having a big kick-off mixer tomorrow night. Everyone who's registered at the hotel this weekend is invited."

Then taking Reese's arm, Avery drew her toward a table in the shade of one of the porticoes that framed three sides of the courtyard.

"Sorry, my darling girl. He led me to believe that he was an old flame."

"He was, and the flame went out a long time ago."

Avery flicked a glance over Reese's shoulder. "The way he's looking at you I'd say the flame has never died for him. Hard to believe he came all the way to Haworth House because someone raved about your food. He came to see you, my darling girl."

"Well, he's seen me. And five years ago, his flame definitely went out. He made that clear when he dumped me."

"He dumped you? Silly boy." Avery signaled a waitress. "Bring us some champagne." Then he turned to Reese. "He was your first love?"

She nodded. "First and last." Turning her head slightly, she glanced up at the tower windows. "And not even Hattie has a blowtorch strong enough to reignite it. So if she has any intentions in that regard, I'm giving her fair warning. Charles Dutoit is history."

When she turned back, Avery handed her a glass of champagne and touched his flute to hers. "I'll drink to that."

# 2

WHY WAS REESE BRIGHTMAN at Haworth House?

Mac Davies circled around the side of the hotel and headed down one of the garden paths. According to her agent, she was supposed to be in L.A. working on the cookbook they would launch with her new cable TV show. That was why he'd thought it safe for him to check out the place she called home.

In spite of the fact that he'd sold thirteen episodes of her show, he wasn't completely satisfied with the product yet. It was still missing something. So he'd flown across a continent hoping that Haworth House would provide the answer. It had.

The instant he'd seen the gray tower rising into a cloudless blue sky, he'd felt it—that special feeling he always got when something just clicked. And the moment he'd entered the lobby of the hotel, he'd experienced it again.

Finally. Using Haworth House as the setting for *Reese Cooks for Friends* would provide that special element, that difference, that had built the reputation of Mac Davies Productions. And it should also bring Reese's show the kind of megaratings that the cable network had hired him to provide.

But reaching that moment where everything "clicked" had been a challenge. It usually didn't take him three tries to nail a concept. And he'd never flown cross country to personally check out a location.

The problem was Reese. She'd affected him on a deeply personal level from the first moment he'd set eyes on her. So he'd avoided dealing with it. And her.

Reaching a gazebo, he climbed the steps and then looked back at the hotel. He'd never intended for their paths to cross. In the six months he'd spent working on the development of her television show, he'd made sure that they'd never met face-to-face. He'd turned down her request for a personal meeting after he'd changed the concept of the show for the third time. Hadn't she interfered with his concentration enough?

Now they *had* met. Up close and personal. When the staff member assigned to the lobby door had pulled it open, she'd barreled right into him, and in that brief moment of contact, his mind had emptied and filled with her. Every soft curve and angle of that body had branded his.

The reality of the contact had surpassed whatever he'd conjured up in the fantasies he'd been having about Reese Brightman for the past several months. And he'd had quite a few.

Mac let his mind drift back to the first time he'd ever seen Reese. She'd been giving an interview for her first cookbook on a talk show he'd produced. The instant her image had flashed on the screen, the stir of desire he'd felt had been both intense and raw. He'd felt a connection with her that bordered on recognition.

But he'd never met her before. That much he was

certain of. Intrigued, he'd moved closer to the TV and spent a few moments trying to analyze his response to her. She wasn't beautiful. Attractive, yes, with delicate features and a long, lean body. But she definitely wasn't his type. She wore her dark hair short, and he preferred blondes with long hair. The eyes were certainly unusual—large and slanted at the corners like a cat's eyes. Or a witch's?

She'd definitely cast a spell on him. When the camera had moved in for a close up, she'd smiled, and he'd simply stopped breathing.

Just for an instant. But it was in that same instant he'd gotten that *feeling,* that tingling along his nerve endings that Reese Brightman was his next project. He was going to make her a star on the small screen.

He'd nearly convinced himself that his reaction to her was completely professional when a commercial had flashed onto the screen. Suddenly, she was gone, and the sharp sense of loss he'd felt wasn't professional at all.

Reese Brightman pulled at him in a way no other woman ever had. Instinct told him that she might have the power to pull him all the way in. And that definitely wasn't in the cards for Mac Davies. He'd learned his lesson at an early age. Getting too emotionally attached to anyone led to rejection and loss. So he'd kept his distance.

And he'd been right to do that. A few moments ago, when he'd taken her wrists to pull her up from the floor, he'd lost all track of his surroundings. And he hadn't wanted to let her go. If she hadn't snapped him out of his trance, he might not have.

Leaning against the railing of the gazebo, Mac took

out his cell phone and punched in the private number of Reese Brightman's agent.

"Madelyn, it's Mac Davies."

"Tell me you love Haworth House," she said. Madelyn Willard had been in the business for over twenty years and had a reputation for being smart and tough, but reasonable.

"Well?" Madelyn said. "Don't keep me in suspense. I haven't said a word to Reese about your idea to use Haworth House as a setting for her show because I thought you might change your mind again. Who knows? You might get a yen and switch to the Caribbean, or perhaps the Himalayas."

Suppressing a grin, Mac kept his tone serious. "I hadn't thought of Tibet…"

"And don't you *dare* start now. I was joking."

"Me, too."

"Good. But I know who I'm dealing with. And for you, filming in Tibet could be in the possibility box."

She was right. In the three years that he'd been producing his own projects, he'd gained a reputation for good instincts and taking risks. So far both had paid off. *Variety* had recently referred to him as a magnet for both ratings and Emmy nominations. The network that had bought Reese's show wanted both. With Haworth House as part of the package, "Reese Cooks for Friends" should deliver them.

When Mac realized that he'd turned back to face the hotel, he ruthlessly dragged his thoughts back to the problem at hand. "Tibet's off the list for now. I called to find out what Reese is doing here at Haworth House."

"She's there?"

"I saw her in the lobby not ten minutes ago." In the flesh, Mac thought.

"She hasn't informed me of any travel plans. Last I heard, she intended to hole up in her apartment and work on that cookbook that you want to launch with the start of her show. However, I'm not her mother or even her fairy godmother. You've definitely settled on Haworth House, right? You'll use it for the series?"

Right back to business. It was one of the things he admired about Madelyn. "Yes. The hotel will serve as the perfect backdrop for the show." He'd already pictured some of the scenes, Reese serving friends in one of the private dining rooms, a picnic on the beach, an alfresco dinner in the very gazebo he was standing in right now.

"Hallelujah! Picture me doing a happy dance."

"Once you get her approval and we do the paperwork, I can get a production crew here to start filming background shots." And he could do all of that from L.A. The director could scout out other locations easily enough. He didn't have to micromanage everything. He could catch the next ferry to the mainland and be on his way.

That was the smart thing to do. The safe thing. And Mac had always chosen the safe path when it came to women. Being orphaned at four and separated from his brothers and sister had taught Mac to be cautious when it came to personal relationships. You could lose everything in a heartbeat. His experiences in his adoptive home had reinforced that lesson early on. His new parents, an actor and actress, had always put their careers first. As a result, his relationship with them had never been close. He'd always been an outsider, looking in at their lives.

On the whole, though, Mac couldn't complain. They'd provided him with nannies, an excellent college education at NYU and access to an incredible professional network that had allowed him to advance quite quickly in a career he loved. A career in which he thrived on taking risks. But before seeing Reese, he'd never been tempted to take a risk on a personal level.

"You still there, Mac?"

"Yes."

"I can call Reese about using Haworth House as a background setting for the series, of course. But as long as you're right there, why don't you broach the subject? Then you could sell it in person and not through an intermediary."

He frowned. "You think there'll be a problem?"

"I didn't say that. But you did shoot three versions of the pilot before you were happy. She may fear you're waffling again. In person, you could reassure her that you're not."

And he could blow his plan to keep his distance.

When Mac said nothing, Madelyn hurried on. "I'm a bit curious as to why she's there. Even though it's the family home she and her sisters have always wanted to build, she doesn't go there often. Perhaps her sisters are flying in for some special event."

*Event.*

Mac reached into his pocket and drew out a brochure that Tess, one of the waitresses, had handed him. It advertised a Singles Weekend. Tess had chattered on about it each time she'd waited on his table, and she'd encouraged him to attend the activities, promising him that he wouldn't be disappointed. There were going to be a variety of singles mixing events and even a night when anyone brave enough could draw fantasies out of a box that silent film star Hattie Haworth had reputedly used with her lover.

Suddenly, Reese's exchange with the hotel manager flashed into his mind.

"You're early," he'd said.

"One day," she'd replied.

And he'd mentioned the Singles Weekend.

Then Mac recalled the parchment paper he'd picked up off the floor.... *You will explore all of the sensual delights of having your own boy toy.*

He'd been puzzled about it at the time, but any curiosity he might have felt had been overridden by his need to get away from her.

So that he could think. His frown deepened. He sure as hell didn't like what he was thinking right now. *Boy toy?* Had she changed her plans to come home so that she could explore a sexual fantasy?

No. She just wasn't the type of woman he'd ever suspect of being into sexual...games. That certainly wasn't the girl-next-door persona she projected on the small screen.

"I'll talk to her, Madelyn. You're right—it will be best if I sell the idea in person. Now that I've seen the place, I think it's essential to set the show at Haworth House. I'll reassure her that this is a final decision. That I won't bring in camera crews and then change my mind...and fly her off to Tibet."

"Great. I'll check with her tomorrow before I start the paperwork."

"Right."

After pocketing his cell, Mac made his way back to the hotel. As much as he might be wary of her on a personal level, making sure that he delivered the best possible show for her had to be his first commitment. So he'd stay long enough to convince her that Haworth

House would nail the kind of ratings that would help both their careers.

Then he'd fly back to L.A.

That settled, he climbed the steps and entered the lobby. A buzz of conversation drew his attention to the arch that opened into a courtyard. A small group of staff members and guests had gathered around one of the tables. He spotted Avery Cooper first. As he moved forward, he saw that the manager had his arm around Reese.

It took him a couple of seconds to recognize the man on Reese's other side. Charles Dutoit. He was one of the up-and-coming restaurant chefs in the Los Angeles area—very popular with the young movie star crowd. The man's agent had been shopping him around for a TV show. Mac had even looked briefly at some video clips, but though the man was handsome enough, there was something about Charles Dutoit that hadn't clicked for him.

What was the L.A. chef doing here at Haworth House?

Mac spotted Tess, the waitress who'd been so friendly to him, and joined her at the edge of the group surrounding Reese's table.

"I'm just over-reacting because of jet lag," Reese was saying.

"I don't think so," Charles Dutoit commented. "A black rose is a nasty thing to send anyone."

Mac was tall enough that he caught a glimpse of the rose. A chill worked its way up his spine. He spoke in a low voice to Tess. "What happened?"

"Oh, Mr. Davies." She, too, spoke in a hushed voice. "It's the most horrible thing." She paused, glancing back at Reese. "Ms. Brightman just arrived and she was having lunch with Mr. Cooper. There was a flower delivery for her and I brought it right out."

The young woman's eyes were wide when she met his. "It was this black rose. And there was a note."

"Do you know what it said?"

She shook her head. "No. But it upset her. I heard her tell Mr. Cooper that she'd received two other notes recently in L.A. and they both came with black roses."

Mac shifted his gaze to Reese. She was perhaps five feet away, and he could all but feel the fear radiating off of her. For an instant, the urge to comfort, to protect was so strong that he'd taken a step closer before he stopped himself.

Introducing himself right now and asking if he could help wouldn't be wise. He'd bide his time until after she'd settled. Until after he'd settled, also. Then he'd introduce himself and sell her on using Haworth House as the setting for her show. That was, after all, his goal.

For a second time, he shifted his gaze to the black rose. His stomach clenched. One threatening incident might be some sort of a sick joke, but three black roses and three notes? Could Reese have acquired a stalker?

Celebrity was a multi-edged sword. And he bore some responsibility for setting Reese Brightman on the path to stardom. Two weeks ago, *Variety* had published the news of her upcoming TV pilot. Could that have brought her to the attention of a crazed stalker?

*Whoa!* Mac shoved his hands into his pockets. He could be jumping to conclusions. There could be another explanation for the black roses. Perhaps someone was jealous of her success, or maybe there was an ex-boyfriend involved.

Or a current boyfriend? His gaze shifted to Charles Dutoit. He didn't know anything about Reese Brightman's personal life. He hadn't wanted to before now. But it was clear that she and Dutoit were acquainted. What was the man doing at Haworth House?

A waiter from the bar area moved past him and carried a snifter of brandy to Charles Dutoit.

After taking it, the man turned to Reese. "Here, my dear. I ordered this for you. Take a sip."

When Reese took the glass, her hand trembled so much that Dutoit had to take it back and set it down on the table.

Once more, Mac found himself stifling the urge to go to her. Whoever had sent the roses had scared her. His temper surged. He'd like to have a heart-to-heart talk with the guy. Soon.

Then he shifted his gaze to Dutoit, who'd taken Reese's hands in his and leaned closer. Mac couldn't catch what he was saying, but there was an intimacy in the way he was talking to her that left a bitter, coppery taste in his mouth.

Anger and jealousy were just the kind of emotional responses that he didn't want to have. Didn't allow himself to have. If you didn't become too attached, you didn't get hurt.

A moment later, Dutoit walked to a nearby table and took a seat across from a woman in a wide-brimmed straw hat. Others in the small group around the table also dispersed.

Mac would have turned away then if Reese hadn't glanced over and met his gaze. In the long moment when their eyes held, desire rushed through him, hotter and more urgent than anything he'd ever experienced before. It melted him, skin, bone and muscle. And made him ache.

An image flooded his mind. He was with her in a

very small space, and those long limbs were naked and wrapped around him, trapping him. He had no choice but to take her—to move into her and feel her heat wrap around him, trapping him even more forcefully.

The sensations, the image lingered even after she'd lowered her eyes. He couldn't move. He didn't dare until he was sure that when he did, he'd have the power to walk away.

# 3

*Thursday evening—the day before Singles Weekend*

"HERE YOU GO." A young bartender whose name tag identified him as Grant set a beer down in front of Mac.

"Thanks." Mac guessed Grant to be in his early twenties and he had a tendency to talk in bullets. "Are you always this busy?"

Grant grinned. "August. Height of the season. The restaurant closes at 10:00 p.m. Guests only have two choices." Grant held his hands out, palms upward imitating a scale. "Here or their rooms."

"From the looks of it, there are very few in their rooms."

"Just the way we like it," Grant said.

Mac glanced around the nearly fully occupied room. The U-shaped bar with its richly detailed mahogany panels and brass trim filled the center of the room. In a corner, a grand piano sat on a small raised stage surrounded by a dance floor. Windows lined one wall and, during the day, the ocean could be seen in the distance.

Grant pulled down two wineglasses from an overhead rack and used a practiced eye to fill them evenly. "Some of the guests are early arrivals for our Singles Weekend. Are you staying for it?"

"Yes." And he'd dithered over that decision as much as he had over selecting which venue to use for Reese Brightman's show.

It wasn't just because he might have some responsibility for the threatening notes she'd been receiving. Or the fact that he had a vested professional interest in keeping her safe. Or even that he had yet to approach her about using Haworth House for background shots in her TV series.

All of those reasons were valid ones for staying on at Haworth House. But Mac knew that his decision had also been influenced by what he'd read on that damn parchment paper. And by the feelings Reese Brightman could trigger in him.

Otherwise, why would he be sitting here, waiting, on the off chance that she'd come into the bar? He'd purposely chosen a seat at one end of the counter, between the drink pick-up station and a richly foliaged plant that offered a clear view of the archway to the lobby. If she did make an appearance, he'd see her.

He was glancing in that direction when Charles Dutoit entered the room and scanned the tables, obviously looking for someone. The woman he'd been having lunch with earlier? Mac glanced around, but he didn't see her.

Or was Dutoit looking for Reese? The thought had Mac frowning. The man certainly seemed to have some history with her. Was the L.A. chef here for the Singles Weekend? Mac's frown deepened.

After a moment, Dutoit whirled and exited into the lobby.

"It's the first Singles Weekend we've ever held," Grant said as he efficiently loaded a tray with drinks. "Very exciting. Lots of events to encourage mixing, like hiking and a volleyball tournament on the beach."

Grant leaned closer to Mac. "And tomorrow night we have a very special event scheduled here. Guests are going to be able to draw fantasies from our resident ghost's fantasy box."

"So I've heard. What can you tell me about this box?"

"Long story. Very romantic. Think *Romeo and Juliet, West Side Story*."

"Star-crossed lovers," Mac said.

"You got it." Then he winked at Mac. "According to the local gossip, Hattie Haworth and Samuel Jenkins might have been star crossed, but they made the most of their time together. They created this box of fantasies. They're all written on parchment paper. Not that I've seen any. But they're supposed to be quite… stimulating."

Mac had to agree with that. What he'd seen on the parchment Reese had dropped in the lobby had kept his erection hard all day. Try as he might, he couldn't seem to shake the fantasy of becoming Reese Brightman's boy toy.

Why else hadn't he approached her already and introduced himself? Because once she knew who he was and why he'd come to the island, everything between them would become complicated. For both of them. She'd know he was Mac Davies, the waffling producer of her TV show who wanted to tinker with the concept one last time.

And any chance for the fantasy might well be lost.

Disgusted with himself, Mac picked up his glass and took a long swallow of beer. She was making him nuts. She'd interfered with his ability to think clearly from the first instant he'd seen her on that TV screen, and now she'd clearly sent him over the edge.

All day he'd lingered in the background trying to decide what to do. And he was still dithering over it. The last thing he should be considering was pursuing some kind of crazy fantasy with Reese Brightman. She didn't just attract him on a physical level. She had the ability to push his emotional buttons, also. Case in point—the bitter, coppery taste he got in his mouth whenever he thought of someone else becoming her boy toy.

He was lifting his glass for another swallow when he felt her. The sharp tug in his gut and the way each of his senses sharpened had him glancing up. As she moved toward his end of the bar, she was flanked by two men. He recognized Avery Cooper. The other man, tall and sandy-haired, wore a badge and a gun strapped to his belt.

So they weren't taking the black rose lightly. But it wasn't relief he felt as Reese and the two men slid into a booth almost directly to his right. The foliage of the plant partly obstructed his view, but he saw it as she sat down—just the edge of that piece of parchment sticking out of the pocket of her jeans.

First the words echoed inside of his head: *You will explore all the sensual delights of having your own boy toy.* Then the image filled his mind. They were in bed together. Candles flickered in the background, flowers scented the air, but his attention was on her face, watching her eyes darken, hearing her breath hitch, seeing how her expression changed as he touched her, slowly, thoroughly.

What might it be like to be Reese Brightman's boy toy? To focus all his being on simply giving her pleasure? And making her his own.

"Can I get you another beer?"

Grant's words seemed to come from a distance, and when they finally penetrated the sensual fog that engulfed him, Mac found that his hands were locked on the edge of the bar.

He wanted Reese Brightman with a possessiveness that he'd never felt for any other woman. And the intensity of his desire had been building to a flashpoint ever since he'd first met her.

"Sure," he said to the bartender. But it wasn't a cold beer that he needed. It was a cold shower.

"OPEN A BOTTLE OF OUR NEW Pinot Gris for Ms. Brightman," Avery told the hovering waitress. "Sheriff Kirby and I will have the house draft."

As soon the young woman hurried off, Reese said, "You didn't have to come all the way up here, Nate. Your deputy, Tim, took my statement earlier." She shifted her gaze to Avery. "You shouldn't have called him."

Avery reached over to pat her hand. "I honored your wishes and I didn't call your sisters…yet. Someone is going to a lot of trouble to threaten you. The sooner we put a stop to it, the better."

Avery was right, she thought. Ever since the flower and the note had arrived, he'd tried to distract her with the last minute details of the Singles Weekend. He'd proposed that she end the festivities on Sunday afternoon with a cooking demonstration. And she'd slipped right back into her old M.O., using her work to escape from her problems.

She watched Nate pull out a notebook and flip it open. The flowers and the notes weren't going to go away. Neither was Mr. Blue Eyes. She was going to have to deal with both problems, soon.

She'd caught glimpses of Blue Eyes off and on all day long and each time, his effect on her senses seemed to grow stronger, more urgent.

That moment in the courtyard when her eyes had locked on his, the heat rushing through her system had wiped out everything—all of her worries, all the stress she'd been under the past few months. She'd even forgotten all about the black roses and the notes.

If he could do that just by looking at her…what could he do if he touched her? What might it be like if he kissed her? If she kissed him back?

But each time her thoughts drifted in that direction, panic would bubble up. Could he be the man Hattie had chosen for her fantasy? Was Blue Eyes destined to become her boy toy? And what did she want to do about that?

Those were the questions that Avery hadn't been fully successful in distracting her from.

And if she was going to take charge of her life, she needed those answers.… A little thrill moved through her at the idea.

"Reese?"

Gathering her thoughts, Reese saw that Nate had his pencil poised. First things first. Mentally, she squared her shoulders. "Go ahead. Ask me anything."

"According to Tim, the first note just said, 'Congratulations'?"

"Yes. I didn't see it as a threat."

Avery's brows shot up. "My darling girl, even with your convent school background, you must have thought a black rose was a bit ominous."

"I put it out of my mind." *And buried my head in the sand, as usual.*

"The second note and flower arrived a week later. This time the message read, 'Gather ye rosebuds while ye may.'"

"Yes." Hearing the words conjured up the chill she'd felt when she'd first read the message. But she'd ignored that one, too.

"The whole gist of that poem is about how fleeting time and life is," Avery pointed out. "Why didn't you report the incidents to the police?"

Reese drew in a breath. "Because I was a coward. I didn't want to face the possibility that I was being threatened."

Avery took one of her hands. "My darling girl, you're not a coward."

"I am. When you called and asked me to come for the Singles Weekend, I jumped at it. I thought if I could just get away from L.A. for a while, the whole problem might disappear. Or I could take care of it when I got back to L.A. When I got the note today, I realized that I wasn't going to get my reprieve."

"The third note is definitely a threat," Nate said. "'Enjoy the sweet taste of success while you can. It will end soon.'"

"I know. But I'm not going to run from it anymore. I'm aware that it's a very bad sign that whoever this person is, he's tracked me here."

"Do you have any idea who could be sending the notes?" Nate asked.

Reese bit back a frustrated sigh. "No. I haven't been

dating, so it can't be an ex-boyfriend. As far as I know, I don't have any crazy fans. I live a pretty quiet life."

"There's Charles Dutoit," Avery added with a glance at Nate. "He's an ex-boyfriend and he's here at Haworth House. He sent Reese three dozen white roses this afternoon."

"He was just being kind," Reese said. "He wanted to erase the memory of the black ones."

"And he left a message at the desk asking her to have dinner with him," Avery added. "Again. He'd asked her earlier, before the rose arrived, but she'd turned him down."

"I can talk to him," Nate said, "but it sounds more like he's trying to rekindle an old romance than scare you. How about a rival? The first note and flower arrived after the news of your TV show hit the papers. Is there anyone who might be jealous of your success?"

Reese shook her head. "I know that there are a lot of young chefs who have to be envious. I've been on a fast track ever since I graduated four years ago from Le Cordon Bleu. But I can't think of anyone who might do something like this."

"Think harder," Nate cautioned. "The notes all carry a hint of professional jealousy."

"Sending black roses—that's going to a bit of trouble," Reese said.

"Not too much," Nate said. "Tim checked with Lynn McNally, who runs The Best Blooms in Belle Bay. She gets orders for colored flowers every so often—usually around the holidays. The process is pretty simple. She told Tim it took her less than ten minutes to spray a white rose today. But she didn't know anything about a black one."

"So what do we do next?" Avery asked.

"Watch and wait. I'm assuming that you'll keep an eye on Reese while she's here this weekend." He turned to Reese. "And I want you to keep thinking about people who might have a motive. Start back in your days at Le Cordon Bleu if you have to."

"You could browse through those scrapbooks you keep," Avery suggested.

"Scrapbooks?" Nate asked.

Reese felt the color rise in her cheeks. "Collecting memories was Sister Margherite's idea. She's the nun who first taught me to cook. She insisted that it was important to chronicle my culinary successes. Then whenever I doubted myself, I could just review my laurels. I still keep them." The truth was, she'd brought new photos with her from L.A.

"Check through them," Nate said. "They might trigger something." He glanced at his watch. "I'm going to put in a call to a police captain I know in L.A. and make sure they document the first two incidents there. They can check with your production crew on that end and see if they noticed anyone hanging around your set while you were filming."

Avery frowned at Reese. "I wish you'd let me call your sisters. MacFarland Investigations could send someone here to watch over you."

"You can't. If they knew anything about what was going on, they'd fly in. And Naomi's arguing a case on Monday to get a judge to open up the sealed adoption records on the woman Dane and Ian believe might be their sister."

"They're trying to locate a brother, too, aren't they?" Nate asked.

Reese nodded. "All they've been able to find so far is that after they were all separated, their younger brother was placed in a foster home for a year. In any case, I don't want Naomi distracted—she's got too much on her plate as it is."

"Okay," Avery conceded. "But—"

Whatever else he was going to say was interrupted by the arrival of two women who stopped at their table. Reese recognized both instantly. The tiny and bubbly brunette was Molly Pepperman. She ran a boutique in town and had become a close friend of her sister Jillian. Rising, Reese hugged Molly first and then the older woman at her side, Miss Emmy Lou Pritchard, the local librarian.

"Reese, Avery told us you'd be here. We don't see enough of you in Belle Bay," Molly said. Then she nodded at the two men. "Avery, Nate, good to see you both."

"What are you two doing here?" Reese asked.

"We're checking in early for the Singles Weekend," Molly said. She flashed a grin at Miss Emmy Lou. "We decided we might get a head start, check out our prospects, so to speak. We're also planning to take a chance on the fantasy box."

"No, I—" Miss Emmy Lou began.

Nate cut her off. "You're what?"

Molly met his eyes. "There's a big mixer kicking everything off tomorrow night, and Avery is going to let interested guests draw fantasies out of Hattie Haworth's fantasy box. Miss Emmy Lou and I are going to be the first two in line."

Nate's eyes narrowed. "You're talking about the hat box that was discovered in Hattie's secret room?"

"That's right," Molly said brightly. "My grandmother is coming in tomorrow to run the store for a couple of days so I can devote my full attention to the festivities here."

"Clarissa is coming back to run the store?" Nate asked.

"That's right." Molly turned to Reese. "Are you going to draw one?"

"No," Reese said. Hers was already burning a hole in her pocket.

"Oh, that's right." Molly tapped a finger against her forehead. "I forgot. You must have drawn yours at the same time Naomi and Jillian did. And theirs have come true." She took Reese's hands in hers. "That must be why you're here this weekend. To see if Hattie can work her magic for you, too."

Reese opened her mouth intending to set Molly straight. But then it struck her suddenly that Jillian's friend might have it exactly right. She might not have come here with the idea of letting Hattie work her magic, but the seed had been firmly planted the instant she'd run into Mr. Blue Eyes in the lobby.

The question was, what was she going to do about it?

It was at that moment she felt the tingling awareness that she'd felt off and on during the day whenever Blue Eyes had been near.

He was here in the bar right now.

For an instant, everything inside of her yearned to search the crowd in the bar and find him. To leave everything else behind and go to him.

"Miss Emmy Lou and I are going to work the room." Molly released her hands. "Feel free to join us when you're done."

Reese didn't watch the two women walk off. If she did, she was sure she'd see *him*. And she hadn't yet decided what to do. Panic and anticipation bubbled up. Once she did see him again, she would have to make a decision. She would have to take charge.

"What kind of a Singles Weekend are you running here, Avery?"

The sharpness of Nate's tone had the effect of allowing Reese to refocus on the two men. Tension was radiating off the sheriff in waves.

"Just the regular kind. Lots of hotels and resorts run them. The trade magazines all rave about how they build business."

"Other hotels and resorts don't offer Hattie Haworth's fantasy box and the promise that those fantasies might come true," Nate pointed out.

Avery studied Nate for a moment. "Capitalizing on the growing reputation of Hattie Haworth and her lover as matchmakers isn't against any law I'm aware of."

"It's not their reputation as matchmakers you're capitalizing on. Ever since news of that box has leaked out, the talk in the village is that the fantasies on the parchment papers are all very sexual."

"And what's the harm in that?" He winked at Nate as he pulled out a brochure and pushed it toward him. "What happens in Haworth House stays in Haworth House."

Reese watched color rise in Nate Kirby's face.

"The harm is that Miss Emmy Lou Pritchard, a pillar of our community, intends to draw out one of those sexual fantasies. She's close to seventy."

Avery's brows shot up. "Is there some kind of age limit on fun—some statute that I'm not aware of?"

"No." Nate glanced toward the two women, and it was then that it clicked for Reese. Nate Kirby wasn't upset that Miss Emmy Lou was going to draw out a fantasy.

He was worried about Molly. Jillian had mentioned to her that Nate and Molly had a history.

"No," Nate repeated as he turned back to Avery. "Nothing you're doing is against the law. But just to make sure it stays that way, I want to book a room for your Singles Weekend."

Avery smiled at him. "I had a feeling you might, so I saved one for you. Come right this way."

Reese managed to hide her amusement until the two men had exited the booth and started toward the lobby. But her smile faded entirely as a man slid into the seat across from her.

The moment she glanced up, the blue eyes trapped hers. Thoughts slipped away as her heart leaped into her throat and fluttered like a bird.

"I think we should talk about the fantasy on your parchment."

# 4

"YOU WANT TO TALK ABOUT the parchment?" Reese asked.

Mac nodded. "I've been thinking about it ever since we ran into each other in the lobby this morning. I was sitting close by at the bar," he continued, "and I couldn't help but overhear most of your conversation."

Reese narrowed her eyes. "You eavesdropped?"

"Rude, I know. But I'm not sorry." What he'd learned had finally settled the conflict that had been going on inside of him—perhaps since that first moment he'd seen her. If Reese Brightman was somehow destined to hook up with a boy toy this weekend, Mac was determined it would be him. And he didn't have a moment to lose. Not if Charles Dutoit had come here with the same purpose in mind.

"Did you draw that parchment I read out of Hattie Haworth's fantasy hat box?" he asked.

When she nodded, he felt some of the tension inside of him ease. He knew he was taking a huge risk professionally and personally. He wasn't about to tell her who he was, not yet—there was too much baggage there. He had no doubt that he'd eventually pay a price for that, but he'd handle it. There'd be a price to pay personally, also.

But right now, sitting across from her, Mac felt that tingle of certainty, that "click" he always felt when a project jelled for him. Whatever the consequences, he knew he was doing the right thing.

"Can I see it again?"

For a second, Reese simply stared at him while her head spun and her pulse pounded. She'd looked into his eyes before and experienced a kind of intense desire she'd only ever read about. But right now she saw something dangerous in them, something reckless that she hadn't noted before. And it thrilled her to the bone.

Anticipation and panic warred inside of her. She could refuse. She could get up and walk away. Avery and Nate were just outside in the lobby. But that wasn't what she wanted. What she wanted more than anything was to give in to the temptation to take the wild ride only this man could give her.

He smiled at her, and she felt the impact right down to her toes. "Please? Can I see it again?"

Without taking her eyes off of his, she drew it out of her pocket, opened it up, and placed it on the table between them. When he took it out of the envelope and turned it so it was facing him, his fingers accidentally brushed against hers. Both of them went very still. It wasn't just the flame shooting through her and melting everything in its path. There was also a flutter in her heart that continued to dance as his gaze returned to hers.

Who was he that he could do this to her? And who was she turning into that she couldn't seem to prevent it from happening? Both questions fascinated her. And she wanted answers.

"'You will explore all of the sensual delights of having your own boy toy,'" he read. "I just wanted to make sure that I remembered it correctly. If this is your fantasy, I want to apply for the boy toy position."

The flutter in her heart danced again. And for one long moment, Reese was tempted to fling caution to the wind and just say yes. It would be the wildest thing she'd ever done. Maybe the only wild thing she'd ever done. And he was making it so easy for her. All she had to do was let herself be swept away.

But that had been the story of her life. People had always made decisions easy for her—whether it was her older sisters smoothing the way or her agent negotiating with her hard-to-please producer.

She dropped her gaze to the piece of parchment lying on the table between them. Even Hattie had somehow gotten into the act, providing the fantasy that was supposed to take care of everything for her, not to mention delivering the perfect boy toy.

She had to hand it to Hattie on that one. Blue Eyes *was* nearly perfect. But she couldn't live the rest of her life going along with the flow.

Later she would wonder how she managed it, but she carefully picked up the parchment and slipped it back into the envelope. "You're going a little fast for me."

He continued to look at her for a long moment. Finally, he said, "Fair enough. When I really want something, or someone, I tend to rush my fences. But I can do slow."

She just bet he could. It was easy to imagine those hands moving over her very carefully, very slowly. At the thought, the room was abruptly too hot, her throat too dry. She moistened her lips and glanced around.

"I've never done this, hooked up with somebody in a bar. I don't even know your name."

"I'm Mac. And while I *have* hooked up with women in bars before, I don't make a habit of it." He leaned against the back of the booth. "There's usually a bit of small talk involved. I've put it together—what with eavesdropping and your very friendly staff—that you're Reese Brightman, one of the owners of this delightful hotel. And this is the first Singles Weekend Haworth House has ever offered. It's a first for me, too. I've never been to one before. How about you?"

Reese leaned forward a bit. "Never. I'm here because the manager asked me to help out. Normally, I'm very cautious. I don't even jump into the deep end of the pool without testing the waters first. I'm very focused on my job. My sisters accuse me of being a workaholic."

"I've been accused of the same. When I was growing up, I had a nanny who thought I was too serious. She used to invent all sorts of games for us to play."

Reese found herself smiling. "Sounds like my sisters. Left to my own devices, I would have spent all my time in the kitchen."

"Looks like we have something in common."

She studied him for a moment, totally surprised. She wouldn't have believed she had anything in common with this large, incredibly handsome man. He appeared to be so self-assured. The reckless gleam had faded from his eyes, but they were still very intent and focused totally on her.

She tapped a finger on the parchment. "It's my first experience with fantasies, too."

His eyebrows rose. "Ever? You didn't entertain any even when you were a little girl?"

She thought for a few seconds, then shook her head.

"No. I had dreams of becoming a famous chef, and my sisters and I always dreamed of going into business together. But dreams and goals are different than fantasies."

"You're right. Goals and dreams are serious business. Achieving them takes hard work and perseverance, not to mention luck. But fantasies should be fun. That would certainly go along with the boy toy theme, don't you think?"

She hadn't thought of that before. Reese glanced back down at the parchment. "Ever since I drew this out of the box, I've been sure it was a mistake. I've never fantasized about having a boy toy. Ever. And then..." She met his eyes. "Then I ran into you in the lobby and I can't seem to stop thinking about...exploring those sensual delights."

"I've given it quite a bit of thought, too," Mac said. "It looks like we're dealing with the same problem here."

In fact, the fantasy had embedded itself so deeply into his mind that, in spite of his efforts to go slow, Mac was fiercely battling an urge to throw her over his shoulder and carry her off to his room. Cave man tactics weren't his style. Nor was he in the habit of causing scenes.

But why should that surprise him? The effect Reese Brightman had on his senses was making him different. Over her shoulder, he could see that Avery Cooper and the sheriff were at the registration desk and a third man had joined them. Charles Dutoit. All three of them might well intervene if he tried the cave man thing.

But when he shifted his gaze back to Reese, it wasn't the three men who kept him in his seat. It was the vulnerability in her eyes that tugged at something deep inside of him. He wanted the fantasy—but only if she wanted it as much as he did.

He tapped a finger on the parchment. "If it helps, I have no experience whatsoever in being someone's boy toy. That makes us both neophytes at this. So I have a suggestion."

"What?"

He glanced around. "Can you get us out of here without going through the lobby?"

"Yes."

He held out his hand. "Why don't we take a little walk and test things out? Then we can decide if we want to go forward?"

She narrowed her eyes on his. "Test things out? Like taking a test drive in a car?"

Mac threw back his head and laughed. "No, I think if we get around to the test drive, we'll have both decided to pursue the fantasy. I was thinking more of testing the waters. A walk in the gardens. A kiss. We'll cause less speculation if we find a more private venue."

He picked up the parchment envelope and handed it to her. "I promise we won't do anything you don't want to. Are you willing to risk it?"

She hesitated, but just for a second. This was her chance to take charge, to steer her own course. Sliding out of the booth, she put her hand in his. "Let's go."

HIS LAUGH HAD SETTLED her a bit. So had his intent way of listening to her. At least that was what Reese told herself as they started along one of the garden paths. But to steady her nerves, she tried to concentrate on the details around her. Small lanterns in the flower beds lit their way, and more lights twinkled in the gazebos and the occasional tree.

Once they'd left the bar, he'd released her hand. Though they walked side by side as they made their way into the garden, they didn't touch. Even without the actual physical contact, Reese couldn't recall ever being so sensually aware of a man before. The air was heavily perfumed by flowers, but each time she breathed in, she caught his scent—soap and something else that was very male.

When he placed a hand on the small of her back to guide her away from the path and across the grass, she felt the press of each one of his fingers and she was reminded of how thin her T-shirt was and how little separated her flesh from his.

What would it feel like when he touched her—really touched her? And if thinking about that wasn't enough, there was the kiss. Anticipating it made her knees weak. Though she was successful in pushing the images out of her mind, she could do nothing to prevent the arousal that started deep and radiated to every pore.

"Does this spot suit you?"

At the question, Reese gave herself a mental shake and brought her full attention back to where they were. He'd steered off the path to the far side of the garden bordered by a grove of trees. Nerves jittered in her stomach. "Right through those trees is one of my favorite places on the estate."

"Show me."

"It's dark."

He turned to her. "There's a full moon, and the sea can't be far. I can hear it."

She studied his face. "Why do you want to see it?"

"Curiosity. But I suppose it's also a delaying tactic. I want very much to kiss you, Reese. But I'm afraid that once I do, I won't be able to give you the time you want."

When she trembled, Mac had to fist his hands at his side.

"Okay." She turned and led the way into the trees. And she knew the way very well. He noted that she cut to the right of each tree or fallen branch that they encountered.

"You come here often," he said.

"Every time I visit the hotel. The maze and the rest of the gardens have been carefully restored to the way they must have been when Hattie Haworth lived here. But this part is still the way it's been forever. At least that's what I like to think."

They'd reached the cliff path, if it could be called that. The steep incline ahead of them was covered with fallen rocks. He spotted the wrought iron bench that sat a short distance away. "That bench hasn't been here forever."

She laughed. "No. I had a couple of the landscapers carry it here for me. My intention was to do my paperwork there, but I found a better spot just over the incline."

"You must like to work in isolation."

"I do. I suppose it dates back to my days in boarding school."

"Boarding school?"

She nodded. "Catholic. South of France. When our parents died, the nuns took my two sisters and me in and raised us. I was only a baby at the time. There were always people around—the nuns, a chaplain, other students. My sister Jillian used to sneak me into the kitchen in the middle of the night so I could try out some of my recipes."

"I had a nanny once who liked to cook. I haven't thought of her in years. On the cook's day off, she'd take me into the kitchen and we'd bake cookies and Irish soda bread."

"Did you have a lot of them? Nannies, I mean?"

"Quite a few. My parents were actors, and their work took them away a lot. Employing a nanny made it easier to leave me behind."

"I'm sorry."

"It was a long time ago." He glanced around the area. The moon was full and cut a wide, silver swath on the sea below. Another memory slipped into place, and acting on impulse, he said, "This would be a perfect spot to play hide-and-seek." He met her eyes. "Want to give it a try?"

Surprise flickered across her face. "You want to play hide-and-seek? You can't be serious."

He shrugged, now thoroughly intrigued with the idea. "I'm no expert on the boy toy thing, but it seems to me that playing must be a crucial part of the deal." He took her hand and raised it to his lips. In the moonlight, her eyes were darker, the color of rich milk chocolate, and the urge to taste her was growing stronger by the minute. "What do you say, Reese? Care to play with me? Or we could try that kiss."

She pulled her hand out of his and poked a finger into his chest. "You're it. Turn around and count to fifty."

He did as she asked, and when he'd finished, she was gone. While he'd been counting, he'd heard the tumble of rocks, so he started up the incline. When he reached the top, there was no sign of her. Had she fallen off the side of the path?

*Idiot,* he told himself as fear rippled through him. This was the only problem with following his impulses. The consequences couldn't all be foreseen. There was no telling how long it would take him to find her. Then he caught just the hint of her scent on the breeze.

Glancing down, he saw the wide ledge about ten feet below. The surface was worn smooth and gleamed in the moonlight. Moving gingerly, he clambered down. The crevice in the wall of the cliff was small. Reese sat in it cross-legged.

"You're good at this," she said.

"I could smell you. But you also gave me a big clue. This is the place you found that's better than the bench."

She nodded. "It's a good place to think."

"I can see that." And suddenly he didn't want to think at all. "Still, we should get to higher ground if we're going to finish testing the waters."

They didn't speak again until they reached the bench that sat along the edge of the path. Then Mac turned to her. "I can't wait any longer."

"Me, either."

Mac didn't need any more encouragement. He lowered his head just enough to catch her bottom lip lightly between his teeth. When her breath shuddered out, he ignored the sharp stab of desire and sampled her slowly.

He wanted to savor everything. Her taste—surprisingly dark with just a hint of wine. Her texture—smooth. The movement of her tongue against his—silken heat.

She made a sound, a vibration that shot fire straight to his loins. Then she trembled.

More. He had to show her more. Clamping down on the needs that clawed at him, he took his time, sliding his hands up that long, narrow torso, the sides of her breasts, then around to her back. One inch at a time, he drew her closer until their bodies finally met, melded.

When she trembled for the second time, he shifted the angle of the kiss and let himself plunder.

Reese was drowning in a flood of sensations, of longings, of needs. Her breath had strangled in her lungs, and she couldn't breathe. She didn't want to.

She'd thought she'd been prepared for this kiss. She'd hardly thought of anything else since they'd left the bar. But there'd been no way to anticipate something she'd never experienced before. How could she have known what it was like to have his tongue play with hers? To have those hands run over her, teasing, tormenting, tempting, taking?

And the hunger. She'd never felt anything so huge. She'd never known she could. She had to get closer. She wanted nothing more than to crawl right into him.

Then suddenly, his hands were framing her face very gently and his mouth was no longer on hers. She felt the sudden coolness of the ocean breeze between them. Desperate, she ran her tongue over her lips to recapture his taste. Then she opened her eyes and discovered that she couldn't quite focus yet. When she opened her mouth, he whispered, "Shh."

That was when she heard it, the sound of voices, not close enough so that she could make out the words. Reality began to trickle in, but she had no idea how long it was before laughter registered from farther away. By that time, she had enough of a grip to say, "I guess we're not the only ones who came out here to test the waters."

When she could finally get his face back into focus, she said, "Another few minutes and I think we would have taken that test drive."

His laugh began low in his throat and by the time the breeze lifted it into the air, she'd joined him. He lifted her and swung her around once before he set her back on the ground. "So have I passed the test, Reese?"

She tightened her grip on his shoulders and studied his face in the moonlight.

"C'mon. Let me share your fantasy. Let me be your boy toy."

Totally aware that she'd never done anything more reckless, never done anything that she wanted to do more, she said, "Okay."

# 5

THEY WERE NEARLY AT THE END of the garden path when a figure stepped out from the shadows to their right.

"Reese?"

She recognized the voice before the man emerged fully into the light to join them. "Charlie?"

"You got my flowers?"

"Yes. They were lovely."

"I was looking for you in the bar earlier. I thought I spotted you there from where I was standing in the lobby. Then you were gone."

"What is it you want?" Reese asked.

"I need to talk to you in private. It's urgent." He shifted his gaze to Mac. "If you'll excuse us."

"Sorry, can't do that," Mac said. "Reese and I were just going in."

Before she could get out a word, Mac had clamped an arm around her, steered her around Charles Dutoit and through the back door of the hotel.

"Reese…"

Whatever else Charlie had to say was cut off when the door slammed shut behind them.

"That was rude," Reese said, before breaking into a jog to keep up with Mac as he hot-footed it around a corner and down a short corridor.

"I figure one rudeness deserves another."

She laughed. "Charlie's always been a bit arrogant."

He shot her a sideways glance as he pushed through a stairwell door and pulled her with him up the stairs. "Any idea why he wants to talk to you?"

"None. But Avery seems to think he wants to rekindle a romance that died out a long time ago."

"I'd say Avery's right on the money."

"Then Charlie's in for a big disappointment. He and I went to the Le Cordon Bleu in Paris together. He was my first love. But considering he dumped me flat, I don't owe him anything."

Mac stopped short on the first landing and turned to face her. But before he could say anything, there was the sound of a door opening below them. He placed a finger over her lips and breathed, "Shh."

Reese stared at him, catching a glimpse of that reckless determination she'd seen earlier when he'd sat across the table from her in the bar. The same little thrill moved through her.

"Reese…?" Charlie's voice drifted up from below. He'd followed them.

Seconds ticked by. Finally, the door below clicked shut.

Mac let a few beats of silence go by before he said, "Persistent bastard. He must think he has a chance of getting you back."

"I'm not the naive girl I was at nineteen."

There was a pause as his gaze searched her face. "What happened, Reese?"

She grimaced. "It's a very short, very trite story. Charlie had a lot of charm and I thought his arrogance was attractive. I fell hard for him. He'd been living in an apartment with his sister, but then he moved in with me. I believed he was in love with me. Then a few weeks from graduation, he dumped me, and I fell apart. I ran back to the convent school where I was raised."

"I'm sorry." To her complete surprise, Mac took one of her hands and raised it to his lips. "Want me to punch him out for you?"

Even with the warmth flooding her system, she couldn't prevent the laugh. "No, thanks. It all turned out well in the end. Sister Margherite, the nun who'd encouraged me to go to Le Cordon Bleu and pursue my dream, made a phone call, and they allowed me to finish a few weeks late."

"She must have had some pull," Mac commented.

Reese nodded. "She'd been one of their star graduates before she decided to dedicate her life to God. And she knew the school director, Jean Paul LeBeau. He was the man who took me back, and he became my mentor. He even co-authored my first cookbook."

"I'd like to meet your Sister Margherite," Mac said as he pressed his mouth to her fingers again.

For a moment, neither of them said a thing. She suddenly became aware of how close they were standing. Her back was against the wall, and he was so near that she could see those blue, blue eyes deepen to the color of the sky at twilight. The air around them suddenly changed, growing so thick that she could hardly breathe.

"Reese, I want to kiss you again. When I do, I won't stop."

Heat, a glorious rush of it had her toes curling. "Hold

that thought," she said as she took his hand and drew him up the next flight of stairs to her room.

"YOU'RE SURE REESE is all right?"

Avery leaned back in his chair as he followed the direction of Nate's gaze. They were seated at a table in the courtyard of the hotel that offered a clear view of the balcony opening off Reese's room. The lights inside the room had been on for about fifteen minutes. "I'm betting she's better than she's been in months. The girl has become a workaholic. She needs to lighten up and play a little."

Nate snorted. "That man could be up there with her right now. We saw him hone in on her table seconds after we left her in the bar. They took a walk in the garden."

Avery grinned at Nate. "Good grief. You'd better arrest them."

"There's no guarantee that the guy was a gentleman and just saw her to her room."

"Exactly." Avery hoped to heaven that Mac Davies was with Reese. When he'd first talked with Charles Dutoit, he'd thought that perhaps the Frenchman was the man Hattie had in mind for Reese. But he hadn't missed the flying parchment when Reese had collided with Mac in the lobby earlier. And he'd seen Mac pick it up and read it before giving it back to Reese. "Let's not forget that Reese is a big girl."

Nate frowned at Avery. "He could be the one who's sending her the threatening notes."

"Highly unlikely," Avery said. "He caught my attention when he and Reese collided in the lobby. He literally knocked her off her feet. So I checked him out."

When Nate's brows shot up, Avery continued, "I like

to keep a close watch over the Brightman sisters. His name is Mac Davies. What popped up right away was the fact that he's in the creativity and production end of Hollywood. Keeps a low profile. But from what I was able to dig up, he's the creative force behind Reese's new TV show."

"So she knows him?" Nate asked.

"I don't think so. When they bumped into each other this morning, neither gave any sign of recognition." His gut feeling was that Hattie was stirring up a new flame rather than rekindling an old one. Avery could only hope that she would work just as cleverly at her fantasy matchmaking for a few others attending the Singles Weekend.

But for now, he shifted his attention to Nate Kirby. "You don't really believe that the man who may be with Reese right now is the one sending her the black roses, either."

Nate sighed, lowered his gaze from Reese's balcony and sipped his beer. "No, I don't. If he is, why make the blatant move to pick her up in the bar in front of everyone?"

Avery sipped his own beer and let his gaze stray to a table closer to the lobby entrance where Molly Pepperman and Miss Emmy Lou Pritchard were sharing a bottle of the hotel's best champagne. He'd sent it over himself.

"Since you're being honest," Avery said, "why not come clean and admit that you don't really care that Reese may have found a man she wants to spend the night with. What's bothering you is the fact that tomorrow night, our pretty local boutique owner may do the very same thing."

Nate's beer sloshed over the side of his glass as

he nearly dropped it on the table. "That's none of my business."

"No? A little bird told me that you and Molly have a history together."

"We do. But it's ancient history."

"The bird said you dumped her at the senior prom. Broke her heart."

Laughter drifted to them from Molly's and Miss Emmy Lou's table.

Every muscle in Nate's body stiffened. But he didn't glance over his shoulder. Instead, he picked up his beer, took a long swallow. "Her heart was barely dented. She went to fashion school in New York City, found herself a hot new boyfriend and made quite a name for herself."

"She came back to the island," Avery pointed out.

"When her grandmother got sick, she took over the store. Family is important to her. But she won't stay. She shouldn't. Her dream isn't here."

Nate set down his glass, then rose. "I'm going to check in with my deputy and then call it a day."

Avery bit back a smile as he watched Nate move toward the lobby, giving Molly's table a wide berth. He might say he wasn't interested in Molly Pepperman, but the fact that he'd booked a room for the duration of the Singles Weekend was very interesting. Nate Kirby had never before been a guest at the hotel.

Avery waited until the sheriff had disappeared, then he rose and walked to another table that sat in the shadows of one of the porticoes. "Colonel Jenkins, I'm sorry I missed your arrival."

"Sit down, Mr. Cooper." The tall man with the good looks of an aging Paul Newman gestured Avery into a seat. "I came as soon as I received your message. She's here."

Avery followed the direction of Colonel Jenkins' gaze to the table where Molly Pepperman sat with Miss Emmy Lou Pritchard.

"How did you get her to come to your Singles Weekend?" the colonel asked. "A month ago, when I visited the library and asked her to join me for a cup of coffee, she made it quite clear that she doesn't date. And yet, here she is at Haworth House."

"I think Molly convinced her to come along for moral support," Avery said. "But I wouldn't be surprised if your father and Hattie Haworth have something planned for Miss Emmy Lou, as well as for Molly." *And perhaps even you, too, Colonel,* Avery thought.

Colonel Jenkins picked up his glass of wine and took a sip. "A couple of months ago, I didn't even know that my father and Hattie Haworth had been lovers. And not merely lovers. They were in love—the kind of love that's supposed to end happily ever after. All I knew was that my father had committed suicide and left me behind."

"I don't think he ever left this place. I've given it some thought," Avery said. "And I have a theory."

The blue eyes that met Avery's were very shrewd. "You don't run a successful hotel with a pair of resident ghosts unless you think carefully about the possible consequences. I'd be interested in hearing your theory."

"I think Hattie and your father have shared some kind of existence here for fifty-five years."

Jenkins frowned. "Even during the ten years that Hattie survived him?"

Avery nodded. "Even then. And I think they were happy. Hattie's fantasy box—their fantasy box—is their way of spreading that happiness around. Of course, they were hampered a bit when the tower was boarded up all those years. But the Brightman sisters have set them free." Avery raised his beer. "So I wouldn't give up on Miss Emmy Lou just yet."

Colonel Jenkins' glance strayed to the table where Miss Emmy Lou Pritchard sat. "I've never told this to anyone, but I had a crush on her when I was little— four or five. My father used to take me to the library frequently. And she was there working for her grand-mother. She must have been twelve, but she had beauti-ful long, blond hair. I was sure she was straight out of *Alice in Wonderland*."

Avery hid a smile. If his hunch was right, Hattie and the colonel's father were going to find a way to push them both down that rabbit hole.

# 6

LATER, MAC WASN'T SURE HOW he made it to Reese's room without touching her. Standing there in the stairwell, listening to her talk about her first love had made him half-mad with the need to get his hands on her.

He was furious that someone had hurt her in the past and was determined to soothe that old wound with pleasure. But by the time they'd climbed an extra flight to the tower level and he'd waited for her to punch a code into the door, his blood had begun to pound like an anvil in his chest.

The instant they were in the room, he kicked the door shut and pushed her back against it. Gripping her waist, he moved in close so that every slim angle of her body was pressed against his. He gave himself a moment to absorb the sensation of softness, another to feel the perfect fit. He was almost sure the ground shifted beneath his feet.

Knowing that once he kissed her, he'd be lost, he only briefly rubbed his lips across hers before he began to nibble his way to her ear.

"What about the fantasy?" she asked.

"Hmm?" Mac already felt as if he were steeped in one. Her skin was so soft just beneath her jaw line....

"The boy toy thing? Shouldn't we—"

"Right." He gave himself a mental shake, and he was certain he could hear his thoughts rattle around in his head. Finally they settled. The boy toy thing. The woman had a focus he had to admire.

And he wanted more than anything to give her pleasure. So if she wanted the fantasy...why shouldn't they play it out?

"You're absolutely right. I'm rushing my fences again." He brushed his mouth against hers one more time, then drew back far enough to meet her eyes. "I think it's your call."

"My call?"

It gave him some satisfaction that her eyes were clouded. When he edged a step back and released her waist, he noted that she pressed herself more firmly against the wall for support.

"If I'm your boy toy, you have to decide how you want to play with me. What do you want me to do first?"

Reese blinked, then took a deep breath. He was right. It was *her* fantasy. She was the one in charge. And in a few seconds, the feeling in her knees was going to come back. Then all she had to do was...figure out what to do.

"I could suggest a few things," he offered.

She threw out both hands, palms up. "I can do this. First, you should take off your clothes. It seems to me a boy toy has to play up the eye candy thing."

He smiled at her as he pulled his T-shirt out of his pants. "Sounds like you've given this some thought."

"This is me when I'm winging it," she said. "But I'm

thinking it has to be something like a recipe—one step at a time."

"Sounds like a plan. How's this for step one?"

Reese's throat went dry as he pulled the shirt up and off slowly, then dropped it to the floor. "Great." But she barely had time to take in the narrow waist, the broad muscled chest before his hands went to his belt.

"Step two," he said.

Reese found her gaze glued to his fingers as he dealt first with his belt, then the button of his slacks and finally the zipper. The sound as he lowered it, link by link, was incredibly erotic.

She swallowed hard. "I thought you said you were a neophyte."

"I've never stripped for a woman before."

Reese pressed her hands harder against the wall as he toed off his shoes, pushed his slacks to the floor, and stepped out of them. The briefs that remained were black, and she could see his erection pressing against the thin material. "You're a natural. I'll bet you could get a job as a Chippendale. I—" Whatever else she intended to say slipped away as he rid himself of the briefs.

"Oh, my," was all she could think of to say.

"See anything you want to play with?" he asked.

She certainly did. She wanted to close her hands around him. And then she wanted to—

They'd each taken a step forward before she raised both hands, palms out. "Not yet. Go lie down on the bed. I have an idea." She knew any thought in her head would fade fast once he touched her.

Mac hesitated for just a moment. They were both on the edge—and they knew it. The moment he touched her, playtime would be over. The temptation vibrated in the air between them. The reckless gleam was back in his eyes, and there was a part of her that very much wanted him to take over and make that move.

"You're sure you want me on the bed?" he asked.

"You said it was my call," she reminded him. And she was glad that it was. What would happen if she played out her fantasy? If she gave in to the temptation to touch him—to play with him the way she wanted to?

He leaned down and removed a foil packet from his slacks. "If you're going to proceed step by step, we'll have to remember this one."

That he was thinking about protecting her made something flutter right near her heart again. He placed the condom on the bedside table before he sat down on the bed.

"Lie all the way down," she said as she moved toward him.

"You have too many clothes on," he said as he stretched out.

"Right." Her fingers fumbled at first as she pulled her T-shirt slowly over her head and tossed it on the floor. It was hard not to rush. The way his eyes narrowed and slid to her waist while she struggled with her jeans urged her to hurry. But the sound of his breath catching as she pushed the jeans down her legs triggered a dark thrill of power deep inside of her. She was sure she rushed with her bra and panties, but the sight of him, fully aroused on the bed, and her desire to touch him won out.

"Help me out here, Reese. I'm not sure how many more steps I can take."

Her knees went weak, and she had to push down hard on the urge to simply jump him. But when she met his eyes and saw the hint of humor, she felt her heart take a huge bounce. She had to struggle to hold on to her focus. "Just one more, I think. Put your hands behind your head."

Mac did as she asked. But he wasn't at all sure just how long he could keep his hands to himself. He'd nearly lost it when she was stripping. She'd used the same economical movements she'd used when he'd seen her prepare recipes, and he'd found them incredibly erotic.

He watched through narrowed eyes as she climbed onto the bed and straddled his waist. But when he felt the wet heat of her center press against him, he sucked in his breath and pulled his hands from behind his head.

"Not yet." Smiling, she clasped his wrists and settled them over his head again.

"I'm beginning to think I've unleashed a monster," he said.

"Let's see if you're right."

When she leaned down to kiss him this time, he tried to capture her mouth with his, hoping to hurry her along, but she wiggled away to nip at his shoulder. Then she began a slow, thorough journey down his body. And as she slid lower and lower, inch by inch, she branded him not only with her mouth but with the slick heat of her core. Sensations steamed through his system and burned into his brain until all he could think of was where her journey would end.

Finally, her hand closed around him. And through slitted eyes, he watched as she lowered her mouth. The first lick of her tongue along the length of his erection had him moaning her name. Then she took him fully into her mouth and began to suckle him.

He could stop her, he thought. But his arms were so heavy. And her mouth was so hot—almost as hot as the fire raging within him. He'd wondered how far she could take him, but he'd never imagined this. No woman had ever made him so weak. No woman had ever brought him a pleasure that bordered on pain.

His climax was already building when he finally found the strength to frame her face with his hands. "Reese. I want to be inside you. I want to be able to make you come when I do. And I'm going to need help with that condom."

They fumbled with it together. Then he lifted her hips and filled her. He hadn't thought the pleasure could grow any sharper, but he'd been wrong. The pleasure grew and grew as she matched his rhythm, stroke for stroke, until with one last thrust, he gave himself to her.

WHEN MAC AWOKE, HE AND Reese were nesting like spoons in the center of her bed. His arm was wrapped around her, holding her tight. And they fit perfectly.

As he became more fully aware of his surroundings, he saw a gray light filtering through the gauzy curtains on her balcony doors.

It was nearly dawn.

Waking up with her wasn't exactly what he'd had in mind. He'd never before spent the entire night with a woman he'd made love to. Then again, he still hadn't stopped wanting Reese, either.

Not after they'd made love in the shower. Not after making love to her again in the bed. The thought of what her mouth had felt like teasing and dampening every inch of his skin had him growing hard all over again.

If he turned her over, he could be inside of her again. In a matter of seconds, he could feel that hot, wet fist close around him.

What stopped him from acting on his immediate desire, what had him easing his arm from beneath her and sliding out of the bed, wasn't that he'd suddenly reminded himself that he had rules where women were concerned. What was really motivating him to stand and move away was the dawning realization that he wanted more than fantasy sex with Reese Brightman.

He wanted to spend time with her, to get to know her. And he definitely wanted to share more than one night with her.

How in the hell had it come to this?

Running his hand through his hair, he paced a short distance away, then turned to walk back to the bed. She lay on her side with her hand tucked beneath her chin. Even sleeping, she had the innocence and honesty that he'd seen in her from the beginning.

But she also had the passion and needs of a woman. It was a fascinating combination.

And he had a problem. Thanks to his own wariness, which warred with his almost uncontrollable desire to have her, he'd trapped himself in a great big lie. She only knew him as Mac, her boy toy.

He had to tell her who he was. Just as he had to sell her on the importance of using Haworth House as a setting for her TV show. He hadn't a doubt in the world that once Avery Cooper or that sharp-eyed sheriff saw him with Reese, they'd check him out. Then they'd have a little talk with him—and probably with Reese.

Someone was sending her black roses and threatening notes. And the fact that the creator of her new TV series was here on the island and had used the opportunity to get himself intimately involved with her placed him in the prime suspect category.

*Way to go, Mac.*

Disgusted with himself, he began to gather up his clothes and pull them on. He needed a shower. He needed to think.

And he needed his shoes.

He scanned the area around him, but they were nowhere to be seen. Still, shoes didn't just walk away. Dropping to his knees, he checked beneath the bed.

Nothing.

Rising, he dropped his gaze to Reese as she stirred and then settled back to sleep. His other option was to postpone everything else and just crawl back into bed with her. The urge to do just that, the yearning to simply go to her, was so strong that he'd taken a step toward the bed before he realized he'd moved.

*Whoa!*

He'd already pushed the acting-on-impulse envelope pretty far. If he wanted more than one night with Reese Brightman, he was going to have to figure a few things out. And that would require some thought and planning.

Luckily, he was good at both. Turning away from the bed, he strode toward the door. First, he'd take a shower and change.

A cold shower.

He glanced at his watch. He needed to have a chat with Avery Cooper about buying a little time. He only had one shot at telling Reese who he was and why he'd really come to Haworth House, and he couldn't blow it.

A plan was already forming in the back of his mind when he opened the door and his foot sent a box shooting across the width of the hallway. Pain shot up his leg.

"What happened?"

He glanced over his shoulder and saw Reese crawling across the bed, her eyes squinting against the light pouring in from the corridor.

"Are you hurt?" she asked.

"No."

It was her gasp that alerted him even before he glanced back to see what had so effectively ruined his escape plan.

A florist's box.

His kick had knocked the cover off and several black roses lay scattered across the hallway floor.

Each of them was withered and dry.

With fear icing his veins, Mac stepped in front of Reese, blocking her view as he detached the card. Then he drew her back into the room, shut the door, and pulled her into his arms.

"They're dead," she murmured.

He said nothing, but he continued to keep her close, her cheek against his chest, his hand at the back of her head. He wasn't sure whether he was giving comfort or taking it. The only thing he was certain of was that he wanted to hold on to the moment. Hold on to her.

Finally, she drew her head back and met his eyes. "Let me see the card."

Releasing her, he pulled it out of the envelope. They read it together.

*You never should have come to L.A. Now you will pay.*

# 7

*Early Friday morning—Singles Weekend, Day 1*

TEA. HIS IRISH NANNY had believed that a good strong cuppa cured everything. So that's what Mac had offered to make for Reese after he'd drawn a bath and settled her into it.

Now he needed to settle himself. He had to get a handle on the emotions churning around inside of him. First and foremost, he felt fear, because he had a gut feeling that whoever was behind the flowers and the notes meant Reese serious harm.

Then there was anger, not only at the person who was scaring Reese but at himself. He'd gotten so caught up in her that he'd pretty well forgotten about the threat that had followed her to Haworth House.

While the flame licked at the bottom of the kettle, Mac pulled two mugs out of the cabinet in the small kitchenette. If it weren't for the earliness of the hour, he would have poured them both a brandy.

Leaning a hip against the counter, he tried to clear his mind so that he could think. In the courtyard that morning, his first instinct had been to attribute the black rose and the note to a fan who was stalking her. But the sheriff was favoring a jealous fellow chef.

*You should never have come to L.A. Now you will pay.*

Mac searched the cupboards, placed tea bags in the mugs and located a tray. Reese had come to L.A. to wind up her cookbook tour and she'd remained because of the TV series. The question was, who might have been threatened by it?

A fellow L.A. chef like Charles Dutoit?

The man was an old lover and now a rival in L.A. Other than that, Mac's knowledge of him was sketchy.

He glanced at his watch. It was two in the morning in California, and he knew his personal assistant might just be getting in from a night of club hopping. Michelle was young, detail-oriented and was a fount of information on the latest gossip around town. What she didn't carry around in her head, she could research.

Pulling out his cell, he dialed her number. "Michelle?"

"Do you know what time it is?" she asked.

"I do. But I also know you've never turned in this early in your life. Listen, would you mind finding out everything you can about a chef named Charles Dutoit? We looked at some video clips for a possible TV show a while ago."

"I remember. He owns a restaurant—Avec Charles, one of the new 'in' spots with the young Hollywood crowd."

"That's the one. Can you dig up everything you can find on him, including his early training at Le Cordon Bleu? Also, I've just learned that Reese Brightman received two threatening notes and a couple of black roses while the pilot was being filmed. See if you can find out anything from the production crew."

"Is she all right?"

"So far."

"I'll assume you want the information ASAP."

Mac smiled. "That's why I pay you the big bucks."

"Right."

His mind racing, Mac put his phone away, then placed the mugs on a tray and found a carton of milk. Reese had been in L.A. for six months, but she hadn't mentioned running into Dutoit there. Had he purposely followed her here to make a connection? Why?

Mac pulled out his cell again. The one thing he was sure of was that he had to let Avery know about the latest flower delivery—and about Dutoit's persistence—so that he could pass the information along to the sheriff.

REESE LEANED BACK AGAINST the end of the tub and tried to let the perfumed water settle the uneasy feelings churning around inside of her.

She had to think.

That was what Mac had told her as he'd drawn the bath and talked to her in a low, soothing voice.

She'd been shivering then. She'd actually seen herself shaking in the mirror that framed three sides of the bathtub. Not even the robe he'd wrapped around her had seemed to help.

There'd only been one other time she'd felt like this— years ago when she'd been weeks away from graduation at Le Cordon Bleu and the world had fallen apart around her. She'd run away that time.

Turning, she faced her reflection in the mirror and frowned. She'd come a long way from that young, scared girl. History was not going to repeat itself. She'd come to Haworth House to deal with the fantasy she'd drawn out of Hattie's box. She was doing that, and she was going to deal with the black roses, as well.

*Think.*

Problem was, all she'd been able to think about while Mac had wrapped her in a robe and set her on the side of the tub was *him*. How was she supposed to make her brain function while she was watching those large hands fiddling with tiny bottles of bath salts and oils? He'd even lit candles.

Mac popped his head in the door. "While I was waiting for the water to boil, I called Avery Cooper and filled him in on the latest flower delivery. He's going to give us an hour before he wakes up the sheriff. I told him you needed some time to settle."

Settle? The moment Mac disappeared again, she rubbed the heel of her hand against her chest where the tight little band was squeezing her heart. Before she started to think about those black flowers or draw up a list of possible enemies, she had to figure out what to do about Mac.

She owed the person who'd placed that little surprise outside of her door a big thank-you. If they hadn't left the box for Mac to stub his toe against, he'd be gone right now.

And he might not have come back.

She rubbed her chest again. On some level, she'd sensed when he'd left the bed. But it hadn't been until he'd kicked the box that she'd come fully awake.

She wasn't stupid. He'd been fully dressed except for his shoes and he'd been on his way out.

Her fantasy might have been over.

She narrowed her eyes on her reflection. But it was her fantasy, after all. So she should have some say about who walked away and when.

Mac entered the bathroom, carrying a tray. "I've made tea."

Something inside of her took a little tumble. It had been a long time since anyone had made tea for her. And no one had drawn a bath for her in years. Including herself. She took showers.

Taking the mug that Mac handed her, she studied him over the brim. The bathroom wasn't small, but he seemed to fill it.

The black T-shirt and jeans revealed every line and angle of his body—the broad shoulders, narrow waist and lean hips. Just looking at him brought back sensory memories of what it had been like to run her hands over those lean, hard muscles. The water surrounding her in the tub suddenly seemed hotter, the room suddenly smaller.

She wasn't through playing with her boy toy. Not yet.

"Did you come up with a list?"

She blinked. "List?"

He frowned at her. "Of your possible enemies. Of anyone from your past who might want to hurt you. Surely, you've put Charles Dutoit at the top."

Matching his frown, she considered for a moment. "I was never his enemy. He was the one who broke things off with me. I'd be the one with motivation for revenge."

"Have you ever been to his restaurant in L.A.?"

"No. I'm too busy to eat out much. And I had no idea that he was even in L.A. until he mentioned it this morning."

"I don't think we can ignore the fact that he's in Los Angeles and someone is upset that you're there, too."

Mac studied her for a moment. "Why'd he end things between you?"

She shook her head. "I don't know. It was two weeks before graduation. We'd talked about going somewhere together to celebrate. Then one day he came to my apartment before class and told me he'd changed his mind. He wasn't in love with me and he had his career to think about. That had to come first."

Mac sat down on the edge of the tub and took one of her hands. "I think I will beat him up for you."

Her lips curved slightly. "It was a long time ago. And it all turned out for the best."

"So you're completely over Charlie?"

"Way over. And if someone tried that on me today, I'd beat him up myself."

Humor flashed briefly in Mac's eyes as he continued to study her. "Then why is he here? There has to be something that you've forgotten. Or that you didn't pay attention to at the time. Last night when you were in the bar talking to the sheriff and Avery, you mentioned you keep scrapbooks."

"Yes. They're up in the tower room."

"It might be worth a shot to look at some pictures or mementos from your Paris days. They might trigger a memory."

She took a sip of tea and set it on the marble ledge of the tub. "Before we do that, there's something else I want to talk about. Earlier, when you kicked the box, you were going to leave, weren't you?"

There was a flicker of surprise in his eyes when they met hers. "I was going to come back, Reese."

One of the tight bands of tension inside of her eased.

He set his own mug down. "I needed to shower, get a change of clothes."

"I'm not asking for an explanation. It's just that we never got around to discussing any of the details of this fantasy thing once we took that test drive."

He narrowed his eyes. "What are you saying?"

She frowned a little. "I didn't think I wanted this. I came back here to prove to myself that I didn't have to get caught up in this fantasy thing. When I saw you and decided that I did—that I wanted you—I never got beyond that."

He sat down on the edge of the tub and cupped her chin in his hand. "I don't think there's an ounce of pretence in you."

Reese felt color rush to her cheeks. "I'm not so sure about that."

Leaning down, he kissed the tip of her nose. "I am. Once I saw you, once I understood the parchment, I couldn't seem to think beyond the fantasy. That's not like me. But it's one of the reasons I was going back to my room. I thought that if I put some distance between us, some time, I could think. Figure this out."

As he smiled, Reese felt another band of tension inside of her ease. "We don't have to think right now. We have the whole weekend to figure it out."

He hesitated.

"What?" she asked.

"You don't know anything about me."

"I know all I need to know." She pushed some of the bubbles aside. "And it seems to me that I've got a boy toy and almost an hour to kill before Avery and the sheriff arrive. Why don't you come and play with me, Mac?"

Those burning blue eyes remained on her as he stood and began to strip out of his clothes. She could feel the heat of them as she let her own eyes once more feast on him—the broad shoulders, that long, lean body and the wiry muscles she'd only had a taste of.

Then her gaze was trapped by the one part of his anatomy that had drawn her attention before. "I can see exactly what I want to play with."

"Me, too."

He had one foot in the tub when he scooped up his jeans and removed the condom. Using his teeth, he ripped the foil packet open and set it on the wide marble edge.

"Thanks. I never seem to remember that kind of detail."

"We boy toys take our cue from the boy scouts. Be prepared."

As he lowered himself into the water, their legs immediately tangled. She reached for the condom. "Maybe I can—"

He cut her off by hitting her in the face with a handful of bubbles. "You did say you wanted to play."

Laughing, she wiped her eyes clear and scooted forward until she was straddling his legs. "I do want to play, but I have a particular toy in mind."

Slipping her hand beneath the waters, she closed her hand around the long, hard length of him. "I think I've found it." Then she watched those glorious eyes darken as she caressed his shaft, once, then again. "I really didn't get enough playtime earlier."

"It could be a very short game, Reese." He reached for the condom, but she beat him to it.

"It's my toy and I want to see it more clearly." Reaching behind her, she pulled the plug, letting the water drain until it merely lapped at their thighs. "I'm not willing to share yet." When she slipped the latex over the head of his penis, his breath hitched and triggered a dark thrill inside of her.

"How about this?" Slowly, meticulously, she sheathed him, delighting in the way he said her name on a gasp, glorying in the sensation when he trembled. Each separate response added a deeper layer of pleasure.

Then suddenly, his hands closed over hers. "My turn, Reese, or play time will be over."

Before she could protest, he gripped her waist and set her back far enough that he could capture one of her feet. Even as he rubbed one thumb over the sole of her foot, his other hand scooped up a bar of soap.

"Do you like this?"

"Mmm." She closed her eyes because she was certain she'd felt them cross. What was not to like about the way he was massaging her toes with those slick fingers?

"Or do you prefer this?"

As he ran those clever hands up her calves, the water suddenly became so hot, she was certain she felt the beginning bubbles of a boil.

"Or this?"

He traced patterns up and down her thigh.

"Well…" Everything inside of her melted. Including her brains cells because she was finding it difficult to concentrate. To even breathe.

"What do you think?"

Think? Somehow he'd shifted position so that they were lying side by side in the tub. One of his hands had palmed her breast, the other was still busy on her inner thigh. But through the drugging ripples of sensation, she could hear the amusement in his tone.

Opening her eyes, she looked into his and managed, "If this is a pop quiz, I'm checking all of the above."

"Let's try this."

He dipped his head and closed his teeth on her nipple at the same time that he slipped two fingers into her heat. Then he withdrew them and plunged them in again.

She arched up, straining, and felt a climax begin in the soles of her feet and tear through her.

Mac raised his head and watched, lost in her, as she rode the climax out.

As he shifted and plunged into her, she wrapped her arms and legs around him. "Breathe," he murmured before he crushed her mouth with his and took them both over the edge.

THE KNOCK ON THE DOOR was loud, the rhythm staccato as Mac ran out of the bathroom. He slicked his damp hair back, then checked the peep hole before opening and stepping back.

Avery gave him a head to toe look before he strode into the room. "Nate's on his way, and I've got the scrapbooks." He glanced around the room. "Reese?"

"Getting dressed."

Nodding, Avery turned and directed his gaze at Mac's feet. "And your shoes?"

"They're around." But he hadn't been able to find them yet. He took a step forward. He'd discovered earlier when he'd called Avery to fill him in on the flowers that the man knew who he was. "Look, you need to know I'm not the person sending these notes and flowers."

"Why would you do that?" Avery asked. "And why would you want to punish Reese for being in L.A.? She's the latest star you've hitched to your wagon. Where's your motive?"

Mac nodded. "Exactly. The thing is Reese doesn't know who I am yet."

Avery frowned. "Come again?"

Nervous now, Mac began to pace. But if he was ever going to explain it to Reese, he'd best take a practice run with her guardian angel. "We'd never met until yesterday in the lobby. And I didn't intend for that to happen. She wasn't supposed to even be here."

He paused when he reached the balcony doors. The sun was up now and through the glass, he could see the staff setting tables in the courtyard below.

"Why didn't you want to meet her?"

Mac turned back to Avery. "Because I always keep a professional distance from anyone associated with one of my projects."

Avery let his gaze run over him again, and Mac was very much aware of what he looked like—rumpled jeans, T-shirt, wet hair. And no shoes.

"How's that working out for you this time?" Then Avery raised a palm. "You can take that as a rhetorical question. I strongly suggest you tell her who you are before she figures it out for herself. She's a smart woman."

As if responding to a cue, Reese stepped into the room.

"My darling girl." Avery moved to her and pulled her in for a quick hug. "How are you holding up?"

"Good."

Avery drew back, studied her. "Liar."

Another knock sounded on the door, and this time Avery went to answer it. In the background, Mac could hear Avery welcoming the sheriff and a room service waiter. But he kept his gaze on Reese. Avery was right. She was smart. How much longer did he have before she figured out who he was?

And what would she do when she did? Send him away? Fear knotted in his stomach. That was the real reason he hadn't told her who he was up front. Once she knew, once the fantasy was peeled away, there was a good chance she *would* send him away.

He wasn't going to let that happen. And he wasn't going to tell her who he was until they figured out who was behind the black roses and she was safe.

But gut instinct told him that the clock was ticking on both revelations.

# 8

"AT THE RISK OF SOUNDING trite, this is like finding a needle in a haystack." Avery placed his stack of photos and clippings on the coffee table. When a breeze pushed its way through the open balcony doors and scattered a few, he quickly gathered them up and placed an empty coffee mug on top of his pile.

Reese tucked her own stack of photos beneath the edge of one of the now empty scrapbooks. Each of the five years since she'd entered Le Cordon Bleu was recorded in one of the books. They'd been sorting through the stuff she'd pulled out for over an hour. They'd taken turns exchanging the piles and shuffling through them, and Reese had answered questions. Mac had moved closer to the balcony to take a call on his cell. The fact that someone was calling him reminded her of how little she knew of his personal life.

"We have to start somewhere." Nate glanced at Reese. "An L.A. police captain is going to get back to me if he turns up anything on his end. In the meantime, I have some questions." He took a photo out of his stack and placed it on the coffee table. "After graduating from Le Cordon Bleu in Paris, you were hired by one of your instructors, Jean Paul LeBeau, to work at his five-star restaurant in the Loire Valley. You collaborated with him on a cookbook. Any chance LeBeau was annoyed when you left his employ and went to L.A.?" Nate asked.

Reese shook her head. "No. Jean Paul is closing in on eighty. He's like a father to me. He insisted on sending me alone on the book tour to promote our cookbook because he wanted me to be in the spotlight. He said it was time for me to leave the nest."

"You must have made some impression on him." Mac pocketed his cell phone as he moved toward the coffee table.

"He was a close friend of my mentor at the convent, Sister Margherite," Reese said. "I think they had a history together—before she became a nun. They still correspond."

"I can check into his whereabouts," Nate said. "Just to make sure."

"I vote we cross the octogenarian off the suspect list." Avery straightened and nipped a photo from the top of his pile. "My favorite candidate for the black rose sender is Charles Dutoit. He knew you back at the beginning of your career, he's currently living in L.A. and all of a sudden he's here at Haworth House. That can't be a coincidence."

"I agree," Mac said. "He's been in L.A. ever since he graduated from Le Cordon Bleu. And he opened his first restaurant, Avec Charles, two years ago."

When everyone glanced at him, Mac shrugged. "I called a friend earlier. She checked him out and just called me back. There's something else. A few months ago, Dutoit shot a pilot for a TV series—the idea was to reimagine classic French cooking for a fast food society. It was a play on the kind of thing Julia Child did in the seventies. So far, no one has picked it up. The word is Charles is not the kind of presence in front of a camera that a show like that would need."

"In other words, he's no Julia Child," Avery said.

"He's not even a Reese Brightman," Mac pointed out. "Which could mean he's jealous of Reese's success. The first threatening note arrived within days of the news of her show's sale hitting the media outlets."

There was something in the look Reese gave him that reminded Mac forcibly of Avery's advice. She was already wondering how he might know the specifics of when the news of her TV series broke. Or about who he might know in L.A. who could fill him in on Dutoit's unsuccessful attempt to launch a TV career.

She opened her mouth and Mac braced to handle the question, when Nate turned to her. "Were the two of you rivals at Le Cordon Bleu?"

She shifted her gaze to his. "I suppose you could call us competitors. We all competed within the class. But Charlie and I never saw ourselves as rivals."

"But when he dumped you and you ran away, he effectively eliminated the competition," Mac pointed out. "Who graduated first in the class?"

"Charlie, I suppose."

"And if you hadn't run away?" Mac pressed.

"I probably would have." Reese frowned. "But that's ancient history. What does Charlie hope to accomplish by sending me threatening notes and black flowers? He has a successful restaurant, a line of cookware."

"You have a TV series and a new book deal," Mac said. "And you're getting a lot of attention in the L.A. press."

When her gaze locked on his, Mac read the curiosity and realized he'd put his foot in his mouth. The book deal had just been signed. Very few people knew about it. The first chance she had, she was going to ask him how he knew.

Avery reached over to take her hand. "Hey, darling girl, the loonies are not all in the looney bin. Let's not forget Belle Island's star real estate agent who tried to incinerate both your sister Jillian and Ian MacFarland a month ago."

Another breeze dislodged a few of the photos from the piles, and in an effort to shift away from Reese's gaze, Mac glanced down at them. Then, leaning closer, he gave them a second look. "Wait. These were from different years in the scrapbooks, so I didn't notice this before." Mac lined up two of the photos, side by side, on the coffee table facing Nate, Avery and Reese. "We just may have a clue here. Do you recall when each of these was taken, Reese?"

Pressing fingers to her temples, Reese focused on the pictures. "The one on the left was taken at the reception given for the incoming class at Le Cordon Bleu. That was over five years ago."

"Do you recognize everyone?" Mac asked.

"My classmates. We're all in the front row. But we were allowed to bring guests. Sister Margherite isn't in the picture because she was the photographer."

Stepping over Nate, Mac squeezed in next to Reese on the sofa and tapped a finger on a woman standing in the second row. "Do you remember anything about her? Do you recall ever seeing her again?"

Reese considered, then shook her head.

Mac tapped the second photo. "Tell me what you see in this one."

Reese frowned. "Those are photos I brought with me. They were taken on the set of the pilot of my TV show. The producers threw a party to celebrate the sale of the series."

Nate opened his notebook and flipped it open. "According to my deputy's notes, the first black rose was delivered to you during that celebration."

Reese leaned closer to the photo. "I think I need Sherlock Holmes's magnifying glass."

"Or Watson," Avery commented.

Reese ran her gaze over the photo again. The second she saw it, a ripple of fear moved through her, and she reached for Mac's hand. "It's the woman in the catering jacket, isn't it?"

"Isn't it what?" Avery asked, leaning closer.

But Nate was already tapping a finger on the woman Mac had pointed to earlier in the picture of the reception in Paris. "We can blow the pictures up, but I think you're right. They could be the same person." He glanced at Mac. "You have a good eye for faces."

Reese was still studying the photos. "It can't be a coincidence. The pictures were taken over five years apart," Reese said. "She was in Paris and then in L.A."

"And I think she's here on Belle Island," Mac said.

When they all turned to stare at him, Mac shook his head. "I don't have any more than that. I do have an eye for faces. And I think I may have seen her at some point here on the island. That's what drew my attention to the photos. It will come to me."

"Dutoit is traveling with his publicist," Avery said. "Could it be her?"

"The woman with the big straw hat and glasses," Mac mused. "I only glanced at her briefly, but the chin's the same. So is the mouth."

"Maybe Sister Margherite would remember her," Reese said as she pulled out her cell. "I'll try and reach her."

A ring from the room phone had everyone glancing toward it.

Nate picked up the receiver and handed it to Reese. "Hello."

"Reese, I have to see you. There's something important I need to talk to you about."

Placing her hand over the receiver, she mouthed to the others. "Charlie. He wants to meet with me."

"Please," Charlie said. "For old time's sake. It's urgent. It's about the black rose you received yesterday. There's something you need to know. Is there someplace we can meet?"

"I could meet you in the courtyard of the hotel."

"No." She could hear a thread of panic in Charlie's voice. "It has to be private."

"How about the cliff path at the back of the gardens then? Start out at the gazebo. You can see it from the windows in the bar and follow the path that forks to the far left. It winds around and ends along the path that's open to the public. I'll meet you there in half an hour."

"Yes. Okay. Promise me you'll come alone."

Out of the corner of her eye, Reese could see Mac shaking his head.

She placed her hand over the receiver to block the sound again, then spoke in a low voice. "He says there's something he needs to tell me about the black rose. This is our chance to find out if he's involved." Then without waiting for agreement, she spoke into the phone. "I'll come alone, Charlie. Half an hour."

"You're not going to meet him alone." Mac grabbed her arm.

Reese covered his hand with hers. "He just has to think we're alone. Then he'll be more likely to open up. I'm meeting him on the continuation of the path we were on last night. But it's at the back of the gardens and it's open to the hotel guests."

"There are several places along it where you and Nate can get some cover," Avery put in.

Nate was already on his feet. "We'll take a circuitous route, go through the back of the maze and then follow the path along the cliffs from that direction—just in case Dutoit or someone else is watching. Avery, you stay with Reese."

Nate moved toward the windows that lined one wall of the suite. "From here you can see the gazebo. If luck is with us, you'll be able to see Dutoit take the path. Then you walk Reese at least as far as the gazebo and keep her in sight as long as you can. I'll call you as soon as Mac and I are in position."

"Got it," Avery said.

"And just in case, Reese, I'll need your cell phone."

When Nate held out his hand, Reese got it from her purse and handed it to him.

"I'm punching in my number as your first speed dial. If something sinister happens, punch one and then leave the cell open so that we can eavesdrop."

Then Nate glanced at Mac. "You're going to need your shoes."

"I'll have to stop by my room," Mac said.

"I think they're over by the door," Avery said.

Mac saw that Avery was correct and frowned. "They weren't there earlier." After he stepped into them, he strode back to Reese, pulled her up from the couch and kissed her hard. "Be careful."

"You, too."

For a moment, neither of them moved. Reese wanted badly to cling to him.

"I can go instead," he said.

She shook her head. "I have the best chance with him."

"We need to leave now if we want to get in place," Nate said.

"We'll talk just as soon as you're through meeting with Dutoit," Mac said before he turned away.

As Reese watched the two men walk through the door, her heart sank. She had a pretty good idea what they were going to talk about. The subject they'd never gotten around to discussing in the bathtub.

Avery wrapped an arm around her. "I could have sworn those shoes weren't over by the door when I came in. I know they weren't there when Nate and room service arrived."

Reese recalled that Mac had been shoeless when he'd kicked the florists' box across the hallway. Nor could she remember seeing his shoes anywhere in the vicinity of the door. "What are you saying?"

"Hattie may be up to some of her old tricks." He squeezed her shoulders. "I hope to hell she's keeping an eye on you when you meet with Dutoit."

# 9

"I DON'T LIKE LETTING you go alone," Avery said as they reached the gazebo. "Once you walk around that first curve, I won't be able to see you. And it will be a good four or five minutes until you reach the cliffs."

"I'll be fine," she assured him. "And if something goes wrong, I have my cell." She patted the pocket of her jacket where she'd placed her phone. "Besides, both Mac and Nate will be close by."

The morning sun had begun to climb in the sky, shortening the shadows that slanted across the lawns. The muted sounds of chatter and laughter drifted to them from the courtyard where breakfast was still being served. When the concern on Avery's face didn't fade, Reese said, "If all else fails, I have Hattie on my side."

He took both of her hands and squeezed them. "That's the only reason I'm letting you go. And you're right, Mac and Nate will be waiting for you at the other end."

Yes, Mac was waiting for her. Turning, Reese drew in a deep breath as she walked away from Avery. Nerves still jittered in her stomach. To settle them, she thought of last night, when she'd walked in the same direction with Mac. She'd been much more nervous then. And excited. It was just as she rounded the first curve that it struck her.

It had been less than twelve hours since Mac had kissed her—only about twenty-four since she'd collided with him in the lobby. And her whole life had changed.

The realization had her stopping dead in her tracks. Was this how it had been for Hattie and Samuel? Was this what her sisters had experienced? Suddenly, it wasn't nerves dancing in her stomach. It was panic. She barely knew Mac—and yet from the first, he'd become...what? Important? Essential?

Not the qualities one expected to find in a boy toy.

The panic increased. No. It was her work that was essential to her. Her affair with Charlie had merely been an aberration. And when he'd dumped her, she'd recovered quickly.

But if Mac dumped her? The tightness around her heart hurt so much that she had to rub her palm against her chest to numb the pain. She'd recovered from Charlie because she hadn't been in love with him.

Had she fallen in love with Mac?

No, she couldn't think about that now. She had to keep her mind on the job at hand—meeting with Charlie and finding out what he knew about the black roses, not to mention the woman in the photos.

Then she'd figure out what to do about Mac.

She'd started forward when a voice from behind her said, "Stop right there, Reese."

Reese whirled to see a woman step out from behind a hedge and walk quickly toward her. Recognition and fear rippled through her. The woman was medium height and wore her mousy brown hair pulled through the back of her golf cap in a ponytail. In the sunglasses, shorts and sandals, she looked like any one of a number of guests staying at the hotel. But she also resembled the woman Mac had pointed out in the photos. And picturing her in the big hat and the fancier clothes, Reese could also recognize the woman Charlie had introduced as his publicist.

But it was hard to keep her gaze on the woman's face and off the gun that she carried in her hand. "You're Charlie's publicist."

"Not exactly. I'm Charles's older sister Chantal. I often pose as his publicist or his manager because it allows me to keep a low profile when I have to step in and keep his career on track. Now, raise your hands, please, and move along across the grass."

The woman's tone was conversational and polite, a stark contrast to the businesslike gesture she made with the gun. Reese heard a buzzing in her ears that she recognized as fear. She tried to ignore it just as she was trying to ignore the gun.

"Your hands?"

Reese raised them but she didn't move. She had to keep Chantal talking. "Charlie lived with you in Paris, right?"

"Yes. I should have killed you then."

*Kill?* Reese thought giddily. Was she mad? When Chantal took her sunglasses off and Reese saw her eyes for the first time, she had her answer. She wanted to run, but she didn't dare. *Just keep talking.*

"Why would you want to kill me?"

"Don't pretend you don't know." Chantal's eyes narrowed and any trace of pleasantness drained from her tone. "You're beginning to ruin my brother's chances just as you did at Le Cordon Bleu."

"Ruin?"

"Don't pretend innocence," she said, her voice rising. "First you lured him away from me and then you became LeBeau's favorite. You might have fooled Charles, but you never fooled me. Charles had to graduate first in his class to get the kind of career boost he needed. When I explained that to him and how you'd ruined his chances by seducing him, he finally came to his senses."

"But what does that have to do with me now?" Reese asked.

"You're doing the same thing all over again." Chantal was nearly shouting now. She drew in a deep breath and let it out. "Now, start moving or I'll put a bullet in you right here."

For a moment, Reese stood frozen to the spot. Even her mind seemed paralyzed, which was making it hard to sort through her options. Would Nate or Mac even hear her if she screamed? And Avery must be back at the hotel by now.

Chantal took a step forward. "If you're thinking of calling for help, I'll kill anyone who comes near us. And if you don't do as I say I have no qualms about ending everything right here. Move or die. It's your choice."

Reese made it, turning and leading the way into the trees. She couldn't feel her knees, but her legs were working. All she had to do was to clear the fog out of her mind and focus, just the way she did when she created a recipe. Step one was to press the speed dial on her cell.

Moving very carefully, she slipped her hand into her pocket and pressed the button, praying that it was the right one. Then she counted to twenty, hoping that was time enough for Nate to open the connection.

Finally, she said, "I'm on my way to meet Charlie

right now. But this isn't the way. If we keep going in this direction, we'll be on the part of the cliff path that isn't safe. Let me take you to Charlie. Then we can straighten all of this out."

"We're not going to meet up with my brother. All he'll ever know is that you slipped and fell off the cliff on your way to meet him. He'll feel bad for a while, just as he did in Paris. But then he'll move on to achieve his destiny and become one of the greatest chefs this country has ever known."

The hint of strident fanaticism in the woman's tone had a chill slithering up Reese's spine. The cliff path was only ten yards in front of her. She had to keep Chantal talking. "I don't understand. Why do you think I still pose a threat to Charlie?"

"Because he's fallen in love with you again."

WITH HIS BACK FLAT AGAINST a tall hedge, Mac risked a quick look at the path that ran along the cliff face. For the last five minutes, Charles Dutoit had divided his time between pacing and glancing at his watch. So he, too, was aware that Reese was late.

Too late. Those were the words that kept hammering at the edge of his mind. She should have been here by now. She knew the gardens better than anyone.

Nate was behind another hedge about fifty yards away. There was no way to signal him without tipping Dutoit off.

And the clock was ticking. What if Dutoit had set the meeting up to lure them away from Reese so that someone else could get to her?

Pushing the fear away, Mac stepped out from behind the hedge and strode toward Charles Dutoit. The moment he reached him, he grabbed fistfuls of the man's shirt and gave him a shake. "Where is Reese Brightman?"

"I have no idea. Take your hands off of me or I'll have you arrested."

Nate stepped out from behind a hedge, badge in hand. "I'm your man if it comes to that. Sheriff Nate Kirby. But I want to know where Ms. Brightman is, also. She was supposed to meet you here about five minutes ago."

"I don't know where she is," Charles said.

Mac dropped his hands, but he didn't step away. He was pretty sure that Dutoit was telling the truth. That had the knot in his stomach tightening. "You were going to tell her something about the black roses. What?"

Charles took a step back. "I don't know what you're talking about."

"You're lying." Mac took a step forward, Charles another step back.

"Are you the one who sent her the black roses back in L.A.?"

"No." Charles took another step back.

Nate put a hand on Charles's arm. "Don't get too close to the drop off."

Mac dug into his shirt pocket and drew out the two photos. "She's in danger from whoever sent those black roses. Who is the woman in these photos? Is she the one who sent them?"

Charles stared down at the photos, but he said nothing.

"Who is she, Dutoit?" Nate asked. "If anything happens to Ms. Brightman, you'll be just as responsible as the woman in those pictures."

"She's my sister. She wouldn't do anything to hurt anyone. She's just upset because I'm in love with Reese.

She's very protective of me. And she explained the black roses. She just wanted to scare Reese out of L.A. She would never hurt her."

"Does she know you're meeting with Reese this morning?" Mac asked.

"Yes. She apologized about interfering. She encouraged me to meet with her."

Mac looked at Nate. "She's intercepted Reese. It had to be somewhere along the path after she left Avery at the gazebo."

Nate's cell phone rang. The next thing they heard was Reese's voice.

"I'm on my way to meet Charlie right now. But this isn't the way. If we keep going in this direction, we'll be on the part of the cliff path that isn't safe. Let me take you to Charlie…"

"I know where she is," Mac said as he started along the cliff path at a run. Behind him, he heard Nate tell Dutoit. "You're coming along. Perhaps you can talk some sense into your sister."

Mac prayed that they would get there in time.

REESE WHIRLED AND STARED at Chantal. "You're wrong. Charlie isn't in love with me. I've been in L.A. for six months now and he hasn't even phoned me."

"Only because I was able to keep him focused on his work. He didn't even know you were in town at first. He was filming the pilot for a TV show. But when the rejections started coming in, he was devastated. Vulnerable. Then he saw your name in the trade papers and caught a clip of you on the evening news, and it started up all over again. He said that he'd never stopped loving you and that he wanted to get you back. We argued, just as we had in Paris. But you're not going to take him from me again."

Chantal gestured with the gun. "Move on."

Reese led the way out of the trees and started up the steep incline. There had to be something she could do. Running was out. The path was slippery and she had no doubt the woman behind her would put a bullet through her without hesitation.

And there was no way she was going to let that happen. Chantal Dutoit was going to meet her Waterloo.

Somehow.

She turned back to face Chantal. "Look, you can have Charlie. I don't want him because I already have a lover." Something stirred inside of her when she said the word. Lover had a more permanent sound to it than boy toy. "Let me explain the situation to Charlie and he'll have to accept it."

Chantal snorted. "If Charles won't listen to me, why would he listen to you? Keep going. Just a bit farther. I think it would be best if you fell right about here."

Turning, Reese saw that she was closer to the top of the incline than she'd thought. Close enough to see Mac come into view around a curve. Nate and Charlie were right behind him.

Fear streaked through her. Chantal couldn't see them yet, but when she did…Charlie's sister was unbalanced enough to shoot all of them.

And that was not going to happen. Suddenly, she knew what she had to do. Ducking low, she scrambled over the top of the incline, then stumbled down the other side.

"No!" Chantal screamed. "Stop!"

With rocks shifting and sliding beneath her feet, Reese raced forward. Just another few feet. When she spotted the ledge below her, there was no time to stop, no time to climb down. No time to think. She simply leapt over the side of the cliff.

MAC'S HEART SIMPLY STOPPED when the shot rang out and Reese disappeared. One second she was there on the cliff path, and the next she was gone.

When the woman with the gun appeared at the top of the incline, he had forty feet to go. She was much closer to the spot where Reese had jumped.

There was another shot, and rocks splintered just ahead of him on the path. He jumped over them.

"Stop!" she screamed. "Don't come any closer! I have to finish this!"

"Chantal!" Charles's voice held panic.

"Drop the gun," Nate shouted.

Twenty feet to go.

Two shots rang out in quick succession. Mac felt the heat of a bullet whip past him.

"You've shot her! You've shot my sister!" Charles shouted at Nate, who was standing there alert, gun raised.

In his peripheral vision, Mac saw the woman on the incline crumple to the ground just as he skidded to a stop on the path where he'd last seen Reese.

But it wasn't Reese he saw on the ledge of rock below him. It was two almost transparent figures standing there as if guarding the small cave. He could have sworn they smiled up at him before they faded into the sunlight.

"Reese?"

He saw her hand appear. Just her hand. Suddenly, his heart started to beat again. "Stay where you are."

He shifted his gaze to the cliff path and saw Nate and Charles kneeling over the body of the woman. Then he climbed down to the ledge and dragged Reese close. "Are you all right?"

"I'm fine. Did you see them? Hattie and Samuel?" she asked as she wrapped her arms around him.

"I saw them."

"They were waiting for me when I jumped. I might not have made it without them."

He gathered her into his arms and just held on for a very long time.

MAC COULDN'T FIND REESE anywhere. It was his second trip to the lobby, and he once more scanned the crowd that was still in line to register. Avery stood behind the counter smiling and inviting each guest to attend the Singles Mixer in the bar that night.

Haworth House seemed to have bounced back to normal. He hadn't. Mac ran a hand through his hair. He wasn't sure he wanted normal anymore. He wanted Reese.

The last time he'd seen her was less than an hour ago when they'd stood at the hotel's entrance and watched Charles Dutoit climb into the ambulance that would transport his sister to the clinic in town. Chantal was going to be all right.

Charles had hired an attorney who was flying in from Los Angeles, and the whole time the medics had been loading his sister into the ambulance, Charles had been bending Nate's ear about getting his sister the kind of help she so obviously needed. Clearly, she wasn't in her right mind.

In Mac's opinion, they both needed help. He hadn't envied Nate when he'd driven off behind the ambulance.

As the vehicles had pulled away, he'd looked for Reese. But she'd vanished as completely as those two apparitions had on the rock ledge. One of the staff members had told him that she'd gotten a call on her cell and hurried back into the lobby.

That was when the panic had set in. Because there was a good chance that the call had been from her agent, Madelyn Willard. That was what they'd arranged yesterday. He would sell Reese on the idea of using Haworth House for background shots, and then Madelyn would call this morning to finalize the details.

Reese could very well know who he was by now. And she'd have questions. He needed to find her and explain. They needed to talk.

The lobby was the first place he'd checked, but there'd been no sign of her. No one had even remembered seeing her.

Panic was now a steady thrum in his blood as he'd called her cell.

No answer.

He tried her room next. She hadn't answered the hotel phone, nor had she answered his knock.

The next place he'd checked was the cliff path. He'd even climbed down into the little cave to make sure. But she hadn't been there either.

"Looking for someone?"

Mac turned to find Avery at his side. "I can't find her. We were watching Nate and the ambulance pull away, and she disappeared. The most I've been able to learn is that she took a call on her cell."

"Try the tower room. She told me she was going there to talk with Hattie. She wants to deal with the fantasy that she drew out of Hattie's box once and for all."

Talk with Hattie. Deal with the fantasy. Not the words he wanted to hear. Mac shoved down a new spike of panic. "I have to talk to her first." Because he knew exactly what he wanted to do about the fantasy.

Whirling, Mac nearly collided with a couple before he took the lobby stairs two at a time. He didn't see the wide smile that blossomed on Avery's face.

IN THE TOWER ROOM, REESE faced her image in the mirror. It had been fifteen months since she'd stood in front of the beveled glass with her sisters and toasted their purchase of Haworth House with champagne.

Fifteen months since she'd drawn the boy toy fantasy out of Hattie's box. And hardly more than twenty-four hours since she'd told Hattie she wasn't going to be pushed into anything. She was going to take charge of her life...*and* her fantasy.

Slipping the parchment paper out of her pocket, she stared down at it. Well, she'd certainly taken charge.

Drawing in a deep breath, she looked into the mirror. "I came up here to talk to you about this fantasy thing."

Nothing.

She lifted her chin. "I didn't want it. And maybe I was resentful because I felt you were pushing me into something. But I'm not going to apologize. Because I was right. I don't want the fantasy."

Nothing.

Panic threatened to bubble up and Reese shoved it down hard. It wouldn't help to give into it. Instead, she set the envelope on a nearby table and frowned into the glass.

"Look, I know you've done a lot already. You saved my life. Maybe Mac's, too. But I didn't ask for the fantasy—this boy toy thing. And then, when I saw Mac, I did. So much that I didn't even try to find out anything about him. And now that I know who he is…I mean, he's a Hollywood producer. Maybe this isn't his first shot at being a boy toy. I don't know what to think, what to do."

She was babbling. How did she expect Hattie and Samuel to help her if she didn't give them a chance. She waited a full five beats, then fisted her hands on her hips and tapped a foot impatiently. "Well? You're the ones who stuck me with the fantasy, I think you should help me figure out where to go from here."

This time she thought she saw a shimmer in the mirror.

"Maybe I could give you some direction instead."

She whirled to see Mac standing at the head of the stairs.

Panic threatened again, but it would have had to fight past the nerves knotting in her stomach. She wasn't ready to talk to him. She didn't have a plan.

And he shouldn't be here.

"How did you get in?" She frowned at him. "Did Avery give you the code?"

Mac shook his head. "The door opened the instant I touched the handle."

"Hattie," she said.

He hoped to God that Hattie was on his side. He'd made it to the top of the stairs, but ever since he'd heard her say that she didn't want the fantasy, fear had frozen him to the spot. "I couldn't help but overhear some of what you were saying to Hattie and Samuel."

"You eavesdropped. Again."

"Yeah. And I won't apologize for that. But I am sorry that I didn't tell you who I was right from the beginning. I got caught up in the fantasy."

"Me, too…but—"

"No." He finally got his feet unglued and moved forward. "Don't say any more until I finish." When he reached her, he took her hands in his. The fact that she didn't pull away eased some of his panic.

He still didn't have a clue what to say to her. But he felt he owed her honesty. "My life was just fine before I met you. Or I thought it was."

"Me, too. I was very happy with my life—except for a finicky producer who couldn't make up his mind about my television show."

"Touché. I told you the truth about the boy toy thing. I was new at it. I've never done anything like this before."

She said nothing.

Okay. He needed a new tack. Out of the corner of his eye, he caught sight of the parchment envelope on a nearby table and suddenly it came to him. "We've had a pretty fast ride, Reese. And since you didn't know who I was when we started all this, I think we should start over."

She simply stared at him.

Panic threatened again. "That's what I had to do every time I tried to find the right artistic venue for your show."

Finally, she nodded, her eyes steady on his. "As I recall, you started that over three times."

"Because I like to get it right. But I couldn't seem to do that with you. Even the pilot we sold wasn't perfect. That's why I came here, hoping to find the answer. And I did. I want to use Haworth House as the setting for *Reese Cooks for Friends*. As soon as I got here, something clicked. I knew it would be perfect."

"I could have told you that. I made an appointment

to suggest we use Haworth House, but you wouldn't see me."

"Because I was afraid. I was so afraid of what I was feeling for you even then. But if I hadn't come here, I might never have found you."

He kept one of her hands in his as he drew her over to the table. "With you, I need to get everything perfect. I'd like you to read your fantasy to me again."

Her eyes narrowed briefly on his before she released his hand, picked up the envelope and pulled the parchment out. "You will explore all of the sensual delights of having your own boy toy."

Mac snagged her hand and dropped to one knee. "If this is your fantasy, I want to apply for the job again. But this time, I want more than a weekend. And I want you to know that being with you is more than a fantasy to me. It's become my dream."

Reese stared at him. "Your dream?"

"We agreed there's a difference. Remember?"

She nodded.

"I want a chance to achieve my dream. I love you. So if I can't get it right the first time, if either of us is unhappy with the results, I want unlimited chances to start over."

She dropped to her knees.

He saw the tears brimming in her eyes and panic bubbled up again.

"What if you do get it right?" she asked. "What if you already have?"

He smiled at her. And framing her face with his hands, he brushed away the escaping tears with his thumbs. "Well, there's always something to be tweaked. You know me. I figure there's got to be something we can work on."

"As long as we're working on it together."

"Exactly."

"I love you, too, Mac." She smiled at him then. "But you may still be going just a little too fast for me. I think we should take a test drive."

"Excellent idea."

She was already pulling his shirt off.

"I think I'm going to enjoy working with you, Reese Brightman."

"Don't jump to any rash conclusions," she cautioned as she threaded her hands into his hair and drew his mouth close to hers. "We can always start over."

As their lips met, melded, mated, they both heard it—a shimmer of satisfied laughter.

# SAVING BRIE

## 1

*11:30 a.m. Friday—Singles Weekend, Day 1*

BRIE SULLIVAN AWOKE SLOWLY, absorbing each separate detail as she moved through the layers of sleep. There was the hum of a motor, the muted sound of a bluesy sax and it was daylight.

Where was she?

Opening her eyes, she blinked at the sun's rays flooding the car, then squeezed her eyes shut again.

She knew exactly where she was. She'd needed only that one quick glimpse of the man in the driver's seat to bring all the grim details flooding back.

He was ex-CIA agent Cody Marsh, the man charged with keeping her alive, a man who'd practically kidnapped her off the street in Times Square and eventually whisked her away in his car.

Not that she'd objected to being whisked. She'd gone along with him quite willingly after someone had taken a shot at her.

Brie had no idea how long she'd slept, but she'd badly needed the brief escape from the nightmare that had become her life. Now reality was back with a vengeance. Cody Marsh was the second man who'd been assigned the task of making sure she survived long enough to testify at Dicky Ferrante's trial in New York City.

Her first bodyguard was dead.

When he'd escorted her to the Kansas City airport yesterday, he'd taken a bullet meant for her. She'd run for her life and when she'd used the special phone she'd been given for emergencies, Federal Marshal Maxine Norville, the agent who was in charge of her case, had flown out in person to bring her safely back to the Big Apple. But Maxine suspected there was a leak in her office. So she'd put in a call to Cody Marsh. Maxine had explained that while his methods might be unorthodox, he was unparalleled at providing security.

Well, the events of the last twenty-four hours had proven that if there was one thing Brie needed, it was excellent security.

So far Cody Marsh had delivered in spades. Dodging bullets in Times Square seemed to be right up his alley. And she felt safe with him—safer than she'd felt in the six months since she'd left her place of work, a classy bar on the Upper East Side of New York, and stepped into a pile of trouble.

The Dark Horse Tavern had been her best singing gig in over a year, and her agent had just booked her into a lounge at a newly opened casino in Las Vegas. Everything had been coming up roses for Brie Sullivan.

Until she'd stepped into that alley and witnessed up-and-coming mobster, Dicky Ferrante, gun down her boss.

Talk about being in the wrong place at the wrong time. Dicky had taken a shot at her, too, before she'd high-tailed it out of there using all the skill she'd picked up as a state-wide champion in track. Then she'd played the good citizen and reported the shooting to the police.

After that, life as she'd known it had gone to hell in a handbag. She'd been put into the witness protection program, shipped off to a small town in Kansas where she'd been waiting tables for six months, biding her time until Dicky's trial. That was going to happen on Monday. Then her goal was to get her old life back.

And Cody Marsh just might be her ticket for doing that. He'd certainly handled the situation well in Times Square. The instant a bullet had shattered the glass window behind them, he'd grabbed her and dragged her away from the scene.

There'd been screams, Maxine Norville's among them. The marshal had been calling to them to come back. But Cody Marsh had heeded no one as he'd propelled her through a hotel lobby, out a back entrance and into the first taxi he'd found.

Now she was in a car with him. Her life was in the hands of a man she knew nothing about.

Except for one thing.

For some reason she could not fathom, she was incredibly attracted to him. Then again, her initial response to him might have been some kind of aberration induced by two close brushes with death.

That was what she was hoping for.

But there was only one way to find out.

The first step was to open her eyes. She did so slowly this time, squinting against the sunlight. It had been barely dawn when they'd left New York.

She glanced out the window rather than look directly at Cody. She wasn't quite ready to do that yet. Brie studied the tall grass growing at the side of the road and the rocks and boulders beyond them. When they rounded a curve, she caught a glimpse of a sparkling blue sea. "I'm definitely not in Kansas anymore."

Cody chuckled. "Definitely not. You're in Maine."

The sound of his voice sent a ripple of awareness along her nerve endings.

Oh-oh. There went her aberration theory. She was very tempted to look at him because he'd be smiling. And the man had a killer smile. She'd gotten one brief glimpse of it before all hell had broken loose. Instead, she focused on a gull winging its way into a clear blue sky. "Where are we going?"

"A small hotel on an isolated island off the coast. Haworth House. I know the manager, and an old colleague of mine from the CIA is engaged to one of the owners. I did him a favor a while back, and ever since then, I can visit Haworth House whenever I want. I called ahead to book the room and told them I'd be bringing my fiancée."

Brie's head took a little spin, but she kept her gaze on the road. "You told them I'm your fiancée?"

"It's our cover story for the weekend. There'll be less speculation about our sharing a room."

"We'll be sharing a room?" Brie could have bitten her tongue. She was beginning to sound like a parrot. And that wasn't her style at all. Though she still didn't glance at him, she felt the heat of his gaze.

"Until I deliver you to court in New York City on Monday and you testify against Dicky Ferrante, we're going to be together twenty-four-seven. No one, not even Maxine Norville, knows where we're headed. I don't expect any problems, but I like to be prepared. So I'm not letting you out of my sight."

Brie managed to keep her gaze fixed on the road

ahead, but she couldn't do a thing to prevent the thrill that moved through her.

*Get a grip,* she told herself. She shouldn't be thinking about the possible side benefits of sharing a room with Cody Marsh. Didn't she have enough on her plate right now?

And it wasn't like her to be so…what? So quickly taken with a man? Sure, instant chemistry, sexual attraction were things she sang about all the time. She even projected them in her songs. And she was good at it. But in her private life she'd always been cautious. It wasn't that she didn't like men. She did. But she kept her relationships casual, fun. Her career had always come first. And it would come first again.

Gathering her thoughts, Brie said, "I don't have any clothes with me. I abandoned my bags at the airport in Kansas City right after that young marshal was shot."

"After Maxine called me, I did some shopping and packed a bag for you. I think I got the sizes right. For the shoes, I stuck to sandals."

Sandals. The man had bought sandals for her.

"Your little nap aside, I can't imagine you've gotten much sleep in the last twenty-four hours. Once we reach Haworth House, you can sleep the weekend away if you'd like. You'll be safe there."

Brie flicked him a sideways glance. "When Marshal Norville came out to fetch me in Kansas, she told me I'd be safe with her, too. Then someone shot at us in Times Square."

"Yeah," Cody said. "Somebody in her office definitely has to be on Ferrante's payroll. That's why we're not telling her where we're headed. Maxine thinks the world of you, by the way. She says you've been a really good sport about the whole witness protection thing."

Good sport. That was her all right. Brie Sullivan, lounge singer, murder witness and all around good sport. She could picture the words like a neon sign blinking on and off over her head.

A little flame of anger flickered to life inside of her. Brie found it a welcome respite from the numbness that had been plaguing her for the past twenty-four hours.

"You know, that's exactly what Maxine told me six months ago when I agreed to testify against Dicky Ferrante. 'You're being a good citizen and a good sport about this.'"

"That's what she's supposed to say to you. It's her job to get you to cooperate and testify, and she's very good at it."

"Oh, I've been cooperating." Brie fisted her hands on her lap, but she was careful to keep her eyes on the scenery. "And where has it gotten me so far? I've spent the last six months waiting tables in Nowhere, Kansas, I missed an opportunity to get my big break in Las Vegas, I haven't been able to sing anywhere except in the shower and Dicky Ferrante has tried to have me killed twice in less than two days."

"So I'd say the witness protection program hasn't worked out quite the way you expected?"

The sympathy in his tone had her finally glancing at him.

And her aberration theory bit the dust for good.

Just one look at his profile was enough to rekindle every single sensation she'd experienced when she'd first met him in Times Square.

Pedestrians had streamed by on both sides, but she'd only been aware of him. They might just as well have been in a bubble. She'd never been so intensely aware of a man before, and she'd absorbed each detail—the tall, lean body, the handsome face with its well-defined cheekbones and strong chin, the full, firm mouth, and the blond hair that waved over his ears and the collar of his shirt.

And the eyes. They were a dark shade of gray and so intense they seemed to look right into her.

When he'd gripped her hand and smiled at her, she'd absorbed a shock of heat and something else that bordered on recognition.

Which was absolutely ridiculous.

She'd never met this man before. And now, even though he wasn't looking directly at her, she was feeling everything again.

He shot her a questioning glance. "You all right?"

"Yes." She would be, she promised herself. She was going to find a way to handle this. Brie Sullivan always handled things.

"You don't have to talk about the last six months. I didn't mean to pry."

Brie gave herself a mental shake as she recalled he'd asked her something. About the witness protection program. And her expectations. "No. I don't mind." Talking would be good. It might provide a distraction so she wouldn't just sit there staring at him. "The worst part of being in the program is that I couldn't get a job doing the only thing I do well. I sing."

"Yeah." He shot her another glance as he turned the car onto a narrow dirt road. "I know."

Every time he looked at her, an arrow of heat shot all the way to her toes. She'd get used to it, she promised herself.

"You're good at it, too. I checked you out."

She narrowed her eyes on him. "You checked me out."

"Yeah. Before I take on any job, I gather all the information I can. It's a CIA thing."

"So? What did you learn?"

"That Brie Sullivan became your legal name when you were adopted at the age of two. I couldn't access anything before that because the records were sealed. Do you remember anything?"

Only in dreams and images. But she'd always liked the dreams, because in them she'd had older brothers who'd taken care of her. A nice little fantasy, she thought. But in reality, she'd had to take care of herself. What she said aloud was, "No. What else did you find out?"

"Your adoptive parents divorced three years later, when you were five."

"Adopting me was supposed to save their marriage. I can't imagine why anyone believes that taking on a kid will solve marital problems. My mom told me I did nothing but cry, and she blamed me for the divorce."

"And your father? Does he blame you?"

"I never see him. When he remarried, he put the past behind him. But he did help me out financially when I was in college."

"You graduated with honors from a school in upstate New York where you ran track and majored in voice, and you've been supporting yourself through a singing career ever since. That's how I know you're good."

As he pulled into a parking space, he shot her another look. The gray eyes held approval. Aside from the occasional employer and the odd member of one of her audiences, approval was something she didn't see often, not since she'd left college. Instead of heat this time, she felt warmth. The two made a dangerous combination.

"My steady employment may have more to do with my determination than my talent."

"I figured that, too," he said as he turned off the ignition. "It's one of the reasons I told Maxine Norville I'd take the case."

For a moment, there was silence in the car. Brie was very much aware of how close they were sitting. Of how easy it would be to reach out and touch him. What surprised her was how much she wanted to. She fisted her hands on her lap to keep them there.

When he lifted his hands from the steering wheel, she was sure that *he* was going to touch *her.* And she knew she wouldn't do a thing to stop him.

"The ferry leaves in ten minutes." He unfastened his seat belt and turned to open the car door.

Ferry.

*Get a grip, Brie.* They were going to take a ferry to the small hotel he'd mentioned. His mind was on business. And hers was on him. On the bright side, the biting her tongue thing was working. At least she wasn't repeating words out loud anymore.

When Cody opened her door, she climbed out and saw that they had indeed parked at a pier where a boat was waiting. Two cars had queued up to drive on board. Cody pulled a duffel and a backpack out of the trunk and shouldered both.

"We're not taking your car with us," she observed.

"Avery Cooper, the hotel's manager, is going to provide us with one. He went to college with one of the owners, Jillian Brightman, and when her life was threatened about a month ago, I was able to provide some help. When he offered the car, I took it. That way if we have to make a quick escape, we'll still have transportation available here on the mainland."

When she said nothing, he ran a hand down her arm. "I'm not expecting trouble. But I like to consider all the options."

He was good at considering options, she reminded herself. And at choosing them on the spot. After all, he couldn't have been expecting what went down in Times Square. But he'd gotten her away from it.

"One thing I should warn you about," Cody continued as they walked toward the pier, "Haworth House has a ghost. I'll fill you in on the ride."

# 2

To Cody's surprise, the ferry to Belle Island was packed, and the last few passengers were still boarding. All the seats on the upper deck had been taken by the time they'd reached it, so he and Brie had joined others standing at the railing.

From his vantage point, he could see the final car board the ferry. At the last minute, a motorcyclist shot into the parking lot and raised a cloud of dust before driving up the gang plank.

Minutes later, the boat got underway.

"How long is the trip?' Brie asked.

"About half an hour. See that cliff over there? That's Haworth House." He pointed to the tower jutting into the cloudless blue sky.

Cody was very much aware of how close Brie was—so close that when she'd turned to look in the direction he was pointing, she brushed against his arm. He felt the heat arrow right to his center. Her effect on his senses hadn't diminished one iota from the moment he'd clasped her hand in the middle of Times Square.

He'd sized her up before he'd alighted from his cab. She was smaller than he'd figured and slim as a wand.

In person, she looked much younger, much less sophisticated than the images on her Web site. In fact, in the worn jeans and T-shirt, she'd looked more like a teenager than the sexy siren portrayed in her publicity photos. The hair was different, too. In the pictures there'd been a tumble of gold curls, a sharp right turn from the no-nonsense ponytail she wore.

When he'd first seen the images on her Web site, he'd felt that tingle of awareness along his nerve endings that told him there was a strong possibility he'd be attracted to her. But even that bit of forewarning hadn't prepared him for what he'd felt when he'd first met her eyes in Times Square.

They were a bright emerald green with the faintest trace of gold rimming the irises. When his hand had gripped hers, he'd felt an instant connection, and then his mind had emptied.

Emptied. That had never happened to him before. It was a simple meeting of eyes and palms, but in that brief span of time, he'd thought of no one, nothing but her.

Even as her hand had slipped from his, he'd known that he wanted to touch her again. All of her. And he wanted to taste her, too.

Each time they'd come in contact during their race away from New York City—each time he'd taken her arm, placed his hand of the small of her back, or brushed up against her, the desire had escalated.

He'd hoped that while she napped in the car, he'd be able to get some perspective. But the desire hadn't ebbed one bit while she'd slept. If anything, it had increased. In fact, he'd really struggled with the temptation to put his hands on her when he'd finally parked the car.

For one minute he hadn't been sure he'd be able to resist.

Only one thought had stopped him. Brie Sullivan needed a bodyguard right now, not a lover. The lady was in a heap of trouble. Maxine had quite a leak in her office if someone had been able to find out the location they'd picked to meet.

Thank heavens he'd insisted on Times Square, where the escape routes were multiple. And thank heavens he'd been able to jerk himself back into reality when the glass behind them had suddenly shattered.

As Brie struck up a conversation with a woman standing next to her, Cody let his gaze sweep the crowded deck, something he should be doing more often than he was. No matter what effect Brie Sullivan was having on his senses, he couldn't let her distract him from his job.

He and Maxine had worked on a case three years ago, and she hadn't called him since. He'd saved her witness's life, but their working styles had clashed. He wasn't always good at following orders—especially if they might put a client in danger. And Maxine liked to micromanage everything. She wouldn't be at all happy that she didn't know exactly where Brie Sullivan was now. But Cody had no intention of letting her know.

Dicky Ferrante was a man on a mission, a wanna-be mob boss with a reputation for ruthlessness. The man also had a hell of a lot of connections, thanks to his grandfather.

Add brains and an ambitious brother to the mix and it didn't surprise Cody one bit that Dicky had waited for six months to make a move on Brie. He'd probably known all along where she was and then bided his time until the marshals brought her back to New York.

Without her testimony, the murder case against Dicky probably wouldn't go to trial. And the high drama of taking out the star witness and escaping jail time at the last minute would no doubt impress Dicky's grandfather.

Dicky wouldn't give up.

Cody glanced up again at the tower. The moment he'd agreed to Maxine's job offer, he'd known that Haworth House would be the perfect sanctuary for Brie. His previous visit there had been short, but ever since he'd left, he'd known that he was supposed to return. This was the perfect opportunity. Hattie Haworth had already played a role in saving the lives of two of the Brightman sisters. He was betting she'd also extend her protection to Brie.

"There's a big Singles Weekend going on at Haworth House."

At the words, Cody shifted his attention to the elderly woman standing next to Brie. Avery hadn't mentioned anything about a Singles Weekend when he'd contacted him.

"They're bringing out Hattie Haworth's fantasy box at a kick-off mixer this evening," the woman said. "If I were ten years younger, I might take a shot at it."

"A shot at what?" Brie asked.

"Having my most secret sexual fantasy come true. I'm here to help my granddaughter out. Molly runs a boutique on Main Street—Discoveries—and I'm going to fill in for her this afternoon and tomorrow so that she can give the fantasy box a whirl."

Brie shot Cody a sideways glance, then returned her gaze to the woman. "This is my first trip to Haworth House. Could you fill me in on this fantasy box?"

"Well, the ghost that haunts the place, Hattie Haworth, was a movie star who came here to retire after her silent film career took a nosedive. When the Brightman sisters opened the hotel, they discovered the fantasy box that Hattie supposedly used with her lover."

The woman's eyes twinkled as she leaned closer. "Word is that once you draw one of the fantasies out, she makes it come true."

"Really?" Brie asked.

The woman crossed her heart and raised her right hand. "Swear. Scary stuff, when you think about it. But my granddaughter's a true believer. If you're going to be at the hotel tonight, you might want to talk to her about it. Her name's Molly Pepperman. She can probably convince you to try it."

"My fiancé might object to that," Brie said.

The woman shifted her gaze to Cody, then back to Brie and winked. "I understand entirely. No need for a fantasy box when you've got him."

"Clarissa."

At the call, the woman said, "I have to go. Perhaps I'll see you again."

Brie turned and met Cody's eyes. "You're taking your fiancée to a Singles Weekend. Sounds like our relationship is on the rocks."

Cody winced. "Avery didn't mention the singles thing."

Humor flashed into her eyes. "I suppose there are worse ways to end an engagement."

"Sounds like you've had some experience."

"No. Not me. I don't have an interest in long-term relationships. Right now I'm totally engaged to my career. From what I can see, relationships just get messy and make you unhappy."

She turned again to face the sea and Haworth House.

"So you're taking me to a hotel that boasts a ghost who fulfills people's sexual fantasies."

"Among other things. Hattie Haworth also has a knack for bringing swindlers and murderers to justice. And she's been instrumental in saving the lives of two of the owners."

Glancing at him, she quirked an eyebrow. "You're talking about her as if she's a real person."

"Ghosts *are* real people. I've met a few."

"Really?"

Cody grinned at the dryness in her tone. "In the three years since I quit the CIA, I've worked on a few cases involving paranormal elements, and I've discovered I have a talent for, well…seeing ghosts."

"You see the dead? Like the kid in *The Sixth Sense?*"

"My talent isn't that highly developed. But I do occasionally catch sight of people who have passed on. Last time I was here, I caught a brief glimpse of Hattie's lover, Samuel Jenkins. But I have yet to see her. So I was going to come back here, anyway."

"To see a ghost?" Brie was staring wide-eyed at him now.

If he told her he thought that he was supposed to come back, that he believed Hattie wanted him to, he was sure it would freak her out. So he held up his hands and said, "I know what you're thinking. Here I am with a bodyguard who's taking me as his fiancée to a Singles Weekend and on top of that, he believes in woo woo. And it's true, I do believe in it. Hattie Haworth is one of the reasons we're here. In addition to fulfilling fantasies, she also takes care of people she likes."

Though her gaze didn't waver, he thought he saw

a smile twitch at the corner of her mouth. "And if she doesn't like me?"

"Not to worry. She loves me."

Her laugh came quick and fast and it was so infectious, he found himself joining her. They were still laughing when the boat lurched suddenly. He gripped her hips to steady them both and their bodies bumped, brushed and then held.

For Cody it was like taking a shot to the gut. His mind began to empty again, as if someone had pulled a plug, and he struggled to focus. He had to release her, step back, but he didn't. Then he made the mistake of dropping his gaze to her mouth. Her lips were unpainted, soft and parted. He simply had to taste her. Perhaps that was the only way he'd be able to put things into perspective.

"I've been thinking about kissing you since I first saw you in Times Square. It's distracting me."

Truth told, it was very nearly killing him to be this close and not tasting her. When she moistened her lips, he felt more of his brain cells shut down, and he moved one hand to the back of her head. He wanted his mouth on hers.

"Kissing would be a mistake," she said.

"Yeah. We're on the same page there."

But she didn't move. Neither did he.

"On the other hand, it could be an even bigger mistake if I can't get it out of my mind and it keeps me from doing my job," he said. "So let's just see what we have here."

He drew her up on her toes and covered her mouth with his. And what he had was a whole lotta trouble. That was his last coherent thought as the first jolt rocked his system. He'd expected the blast of heat. What he hadn't anticipated was the intensity of the ache, centering in his gut and radiating outward to his fingertips.

It took all of his control to keep his hands where they were when all he wanted was to slip them under that thin T-shirt she was wearing, to run them up her torso, to feel the press of her nipples against his palm. Just thinking about it had the blood roaring in his head.

He had to let her go before he completely lost track of where they were. But first, he tightened his grip on her, leaned against the railing to steady both of them and took more.

Brie couldn't think. She couldn't breathe. He flooded her senses until there was no one but him. His taste was as dark and forbidden as the most expensive chocolate. His smell was a mix of soap and sun and sin. His hands—one on her hips, the other at the back of her neck—were so hot, so…necessary. Her pulse thundered.

And there was so much heat. It had hit her like a blast furnace, and she wanted nothing more than to crawl right into it until her bones melted. Maybe then, the sharp fist of need inside of her would loosen.

A sudden blast of sound froze her to the spot and stopped her from wrapping her arms around him. Even then, he was the one who drew back and set her away.

"We're approaching the dock," he said.

She blinked, but wasn't quite able to bring his face into focus. Still, she managed to say, "I told you that kissing would be a mistake."

"You were one hundred percent right."

The fact that he didn't sound contrite or even worried about it cleared her vision. "This is serious. We're going to have to figure out what to do."

The grin flashed, quick and lethal. "I have several ideas."

She did, too. And try as she might, she couldn't quite push the images out of her mind.

"Since none of my ideas would be appropriate right here, I suggest we postpone this discussion until we get to Haworth House." He grabbed her arm and led her toward the queue that was already forming.

"We have to be sensible," she said. At least one of them did. "We should come up with a plan. Maybe we can get separate rooms."

"I would bet that on a Singles Weekend, the hotel is booked. But I agree we have to have a plan. Let's find our rental car. We'll both have some time to strategize on the ride to the hotel."

Strategize. Oh, good. First he kisses her senseless and then he wants her to strategize.

As they joined the end of the line, he turned her toward him, gripping her chin with his free hand so that she had to meet his eyes. "One thing I can promise you, Brie. Keeping you safe is my first priority."

# 3

CODY TURNED THE CAR Avery had arranged for them onto the road that would lead to Haworth House. They would have been at the hotel already if it hadn't been for the elderly motorist whose car had stalled smack in the middle of the first intersection they'd come to. The only vehicle that got around the traffic jam was the motorcycle that Cody had seen board the ferry at the last minute.

Cody figured they'd lost a good thirty minutes. First, he and another motorist had checked under the stalled car's hood. Finally, he'd persuaded the tall elderly man to help them push the car onto a side street.

He glanced at Brie. They hadn't spoken, at least not to each other, since they'd left the dock.

It *had* been a mistake to kiss her. Of course, he'd made mistakes before. He'd even paid dearly for a few of them. But getting involved with someone he was supposed to protect? That was a first for him.

Good thing he liked challenges. Because now that he'd taken that first taste of her, Cody was pretty sure he'd need a second. And more.

He shot her a sideways glance. She had her hands

clasped tightly together in her lap, and she was staring straight ahead out the window.

Thinking. They hadn't known each other more than a handful of hours and yet he was picking up things about Brie Sullivan. She had courage, and she was smart.

She'd gotten away from the killers who'd tried to put a period to her existence at the airport yesterday, and she'd gotten back in touch with the marshal assigned to her case. If she'd panicked and just tried running on her own, she'd be dead by now.

She could also move like lightning when there was a reason. She'd had no trouble keeping up with him when they'd had to get away from Times Square.

"Did you come up with a strategy yet?" he asked.

"I think the solution to our problem is pretty obvious. We're not going to kiss again. And while we might have to share a room, we are definitely not sleeping in the same bed."

He pressed lightly on the brake and guided the car into the first of the hairpin curves on the road that led to Haworth House. The land to their left had already begun to drop away.

"I can agree to the second. The suite we'll be staying in has two rooms. But I'm not making any promises about not kissing you again."

Brie shot him a frown. "Why not? We're both adults. We need to be sensible about this."

"We're both single unattached adults. That's part of the problem, and what we need to be is realistic. The kind of connection we shared when we kissed doesn't happen all that often. In fact, it's never happened for me before. How about you?"

There was a beat of silence. Then she said, "It's never happened to me, either. And I don't like it."

"Why not?"

"I've got to focus on rebuilding my career." She waved a hand. "This whole thing with Dicky Ferrante really messed it up. When I had to move to Kansas, I missed a booking in Las Vegas. And it took me almost a year to get it. Do you have any idea what I've missed out on? It would have been my big break!"

Cody glanced at her. "Didn't Maxine tell you that you wouldn't be able to go back to your old life, even after you testify?"

"She told me that I couldn't go back to being Brie Sullivan. I'm adopted, remember? So Brie Sullivan isn't even the name I was born with. Maybe I'll try to dig that up, or I'll just get a new name and reinvent myself. If it means I have to start all over from scratch, I'll do it."

Courage, brains and grit. He admired all three qualities. It wasn't just the outer Brie that was pulling at him. It was the inner Brie, too. And that could be dangerous.

"It'll take me a while to get a booking in Vegas again, but I'll do that, too. Surviving the trial and getting my career jump-started again are my top priorities. I don't have time for relationships."

"Me, either," he said equably. Silently, he cursed Maxine Norville for not being honest with Brie. But after hearing the passion in her voice when she talked about her career, he could sympathize a bit with his former colleague. He sure didn't want to be the one to tell her there was an excellent chance that Dicky could eventually trace her if she went back to her singing career.

There would be plenty of time for that piece of bad news after she got through the trial.

Brie turned to him. "You can't like this thing between us, either. It's got to complicate the hell out of your job."

"No argument there. But no matter the complication, no matter how we might feel about it messing up our agendas, we're both going to be tempted again."

"We don't have to give into temptation. We can take precautions."

"I agree." As he eased the car into the last straight stretch of road, he turned and met her eyes briefly. "But I'm not making any promises. The ones I make, I keep. And what you can take to the bank is that I'm going to keep you safe until after you've testified."

Cody shifted his gaze back to the road, which had begun to twist again. To their right was a sheer wall of rock, and to the left the land dropped away sharply. There were no shoulders on either side. As they passed a sign that warned of blind curves, he noted that the cables were down on the guardrails that lined this particular section of the road.

Thirty feet ahead of them a motorcycle shot into view, then tilted and skidded very close to one of the guardrails. Wheels spinning, it suddenly careened into their lane and raced straight toward them.

Too fast, Cody thought as he pressed his foot on the brake and eased the car toward the center of the road. The key was not to overreact. The rock face was too unforgiving, the drop off too sheer to risk going into a skid like the one the biker had just recovered from.

The motorcycle immediately swerved to keep them on a collision course.

Cody increased the pressure on the brake, but he kept his hand steady on the wheel.

The cycle's speed didn't slacken.

Ten feet.

A game of chicken, Cody thought. The biker was trying to get him to panic and jerk the steering wheel one way or the other. Either option might be disastrous.

"He's going to hit us." Brie gripped the hand rail in front of the glove compartment.

At the last second, the man on the motorcycle twisted the handle bars and veered fully into the left lane. His thigh grazed the fender of their car, and that was enough to send the bike out of control.

There was a squeal of tires. Cody twisted around in time to see the motorcycle tilt crazily as it rocketed across the asphalt in the direction of one of the guardrails. The biker recovered enough control to avoid smashing into it, but not enough to get the bike back on the road. Spewing gravel, it shot off the narrow shoulder and into space.

For a moment, bike and rider seemed to hang suspended in the air. It reminded Cody of a documentary he'd watched of Evel Knieval making his attempt to jump the Snake River Canyon. Only Evel's bike had boasted a parachute. This guy's didn't, and a scream pierced the air as biker and bike plunged.

Cody and Brie were already out of the car and racing toward the guardrail when they heard the first impact—a nasty sound of steel crashing against rock. Then came the second.

They arrived at the drop-off in time to see the bike bounce and tumble nearly all the way to the bottom. The rider lay sprawled at an odd angle on a ledge nearly fifty feet below them.

Pulling out his phone, Cody glanced around. "I'm calling the sheriff. He's a good man. I've met him before."

When Nate Kirby picked up, Cody filled him in on the details. "We're going to check and see if the driver's alive. It doesn't look good. I'll call back as soon as I know."

When he turned to face Brie, she said, "Thanks. That happened so fast. If I'd been driving, I'd have tried to get out of the way, and we'd be down there instead of him. You did really good."

Then she wrapped her arms around him and hugged him hard.

The sweetness of the gesture had emotions flooding his system. It wasn't a punch of heat he felt this time, but something warm that streaked straight to his heart.

When she drew away, he very nearly reached out to draw her back.

Instead, he said, "So have I earned back some of the points I lost when I told you I can see ghosts."

"A few."

He glanced around again. "I don't want to leave you here alone. You think you can make it down to that ledge?"

"Of course." She met his eyes steadily. "You're thinking this wasn't just an accident. You think he planned for us to end up down there, don't you?"

He studied her face. When a woman had courage, brains and grit, she deserved the truth. "I'm entertaining that possibility. I also think that it's the same biker who passed us as we were pulling out of Belle Bay, the same one who just made the ferry. I can't figure out how he could have followed us from New York. But when I'm working, I tend to cater to my paranoid side."

This time she was the one who glanced around, and then she moved closer to the guardrail. Leaning down, she picked up one of the cables that lay along the ground. "Cater away. I'm no expert, but this looks like it's been cut."

He turned then, remembering what he'd noted earlier before his attention had become glued to the motorcycle.

"All of them are down," she said before he could give voice to the observation. "If they'd been up, the motorcycle might not have gone over. We wouldn't have gone over, either."

"It could be a coincidence," he added.

"What does your paranoid side think?"

He met her eyes. "Top of my list is that someone knew exactly when we got off that ferry and that we were headed up here. Haworth House is the primary destination spot once you leave Belle Bay."

"They work fast," Brie said.

Too fast, Cody thought. But her mind was clicking along the same path his was.

"Until we find out differently, I'm all for you catering to your paranoia. Agreed?"

She held out her hand. And when he took it in his, he felt that same instant sense of connection he'd felt the first time.

"Let's go find out who tried to run us off this cliff road," she said.

"Follow me." As he led the way down, Cody wished to hell that his gut instinct wasn't telling him that they weren't going to like what they found out about the still body lying below them.

# 4

AN HOUR LATER, BRIE stood at the side of the road with Cody and watched two paramedics load the body of a woman into an ambulance. The biker had been female, and she'd been dead when they reached her. All she'd had on her was a cell phone. No identification.

When Sheriff Nate Kirby had arrived, he'd taken both their statements. Following Cody's lead, Brie had gone along with his undercover story that she was his fiancée and they'd come to the island to have a getaway weekend at Haworth House.

Nate had jotted their stories down in his notebook, then moved back to his car and started making phone calls.

One of his deputies had climbed down far enough to get the license plate on the bike, but there'd been no registration on it. What there had been was a toolbox.

Brie had watched enough TV to know that the lack of identification wasn't a good sign. It made it a lot less likely that the woman was just some poor tourist who'd accidentally lost control of her motorcycle. In addition to tools, the box had contained a serious-looking handgun complete with a silencer.

It was pretty clear to Brie that Dicky Ferrante knew exactly where she was.

When Nate moved to the ambulance to have a word with the paramedic, Brie spoke in a low tone to Cody. "What do we do next?"

"As soon as Nate is finished with us, we're going to the hotel and register. I think it's our safest bet right now."

She might have been a lot more confident about Cody's plan if she didn't suspect that it was partially based on his trust in a ghost.

But she had to admit one thing: so far, he was getting a ten out of ten as a bodyguard. Right now they were alive, and the woman being driven away in the ambulance wasn't.

Besides, her options were limited. Who else did she have to turn to? Maxine Norville had the kind of leak in her office that could have destroyed a dike and flooded a country.

Brie wasn't stupid. No way was she going to take off on her own until good old Dicky was behind bars.

Plus, she felt safer with Cody than she'd felt in a long time. Even as a child, she'd learned that she had to depend on herself. Her adoptive mother hadn't been a bad person, but Denise Sullivan had always partially blamed her for the divorce, and her father had used her as an excuse to walk away from a marriage that just hadn't worked out for him.

But Brie knew she could depend on Cody for the weekend. She'd just have to keep herself from liking that dependence too much. Hugging him had been almost as big a mistake as kissing him. When he'd wrapped his arms around her and simply held on, she'd wanted to hold on, too.

Badly.

There was definitely more than chemistry between them. Or, at least, the potential for more. For just an instant, when they'd stood on the side of the road with their arms wrapped around each other, she'd felt as if she'd come home.

Home.

The only other time she'd ever experienced that particular feeling was in her dreams, when she fantasized about those three brothers who'd taken such good care of her.

Ridiculous. Her dreams of having those brothers were a fantasy she should have outgrown years ago. She let her gaze stray to Cody. He had the face and body of a warrior. A protector. It was so tempting to just lean on him. But she certainly didn't need a new fantasy to replace her old one.

The strategy she'd proposed to him before their close encounter with the motorcycle was their best move. They just had to be sensible adults.

As the ambulance pulled away, Nate put his phone back into his pocket and walked over to them. "So far our motorcyclist remains a woman of mystery. My deputy Tim will run her prints and the license plate number through the available databases. We may also get lucky and get an ID from the cell phone. In the meantime, Avery Cooper says that as far as he knows, there's no one fitting the description I gave him registered at Haworth House this weekend."

"She wasn't looking her best down there," Brie said.

Nate shifted his gaze to her. "True. Avery's offered to run a check on the guests and see if anyone turns up missing. One of my men will also be showing her photo at the two ferry offices to see if anyone can identify her through a ticket. But it will be a while before we have any definitive answers."

There were a few beats of silence. Then Nate looked directly at Brie. "It would help if I could know exactly who you are." He shifted his gaze to Cody. "And what one or both of you have done to attract the services of a professional hit woman."

To her surprise, Cody grinned at Nate. "You're not buying into the weekend getaway with my fiancée story?"

"Well, we don't get a lot of crime here in Belle Bay, but we do watch TV. In addition to the rather interesting tools and the gun our mystery woman was packing, there's this."

Nate walked over to one of the guardrails and picked up one of the cables. "These look to be freshly cut. One of them being down is worrisome. All of them being cut at the same time is something that pushes hard against any accident theory. I was up at the hotel earlier today on business, and when I returned to Belle Bay a couple of hours ago, the cables were fine."

He glanced up at both of them. "They haven't been down long or somebody driving past would have reported them to my office. Those are the kinds of calls I get everyday here on Belle Island. Two attempted homicides in one day is an all-time record for Belle Bay."

"Two?" Cody asked.

Rising, Nate nodded. "The business I had earlier up at Haworth House involved arresting a woman who was trying to kill Reese Brightman. She was just being airlifted to a hospital on the mainland when you called."

"Reese is all right?" Cody asked.

"Yeah. Better than all right, I'd say. I suspect that

Hattie's fantasy box has played a role in bringing her and Mac Davies together."

"Mac Davies?" Brie asked, her mind racing. She knew that name but—

"He's the TV producer who created Reese's show," Nate said.

The memory clicked into place. Brie had read about him in the trade papers where he'd been nicknamed a "star maker."

"And they didn't meet until they ran into each other here at Haworth House," Nate continued. "I'm sure you can get the whole story once you get up to the hotel."

Brie put that on her to-do list. Meeting Mac Davies could be step number one in getting her old life back. She glanced down at the ledge below. Just as soon as she got through this weekend and the trial.

"But before you go, why don't you answer my original two questions," Nate said.

"Have you heard of Dicky Ferrante?" Cody asked.

"Yeah. We get cable news here. He's one of the two Ferrante boys who are vying to take over their grandfather's position in the mob. His case goes to trial on Monday?"

"Brie's the star witness at that trial," Cody said. "Her testimony could put Dicky on death row."

Nate gave a low whistle.

"I figured Belle Island would make the perfect hiding place."

Nate glanced down at the ledge below them. "Not exactly perfect, I'd say. Any idea how your mystery woman tracked you here?"

"Good question."

It *was* a good question. Brie gave it some thought

while Cody filled Nate in on the two previous attempts on her life and how he'd gotten involved.

"So your mystery woman followed you onto the ferry, then shot ahead of you on the road to lay in wait," Nate said. "Impressive."

"Too damned impressive," Cody said. "The question bugging me is how she found us. I've never mentioned this place to anyone. And I used a friend's car to get out of the city."

"They can do amazing things with GPS tracking devices," Brie said.

When the two men turned to stare at her, she swallowed hard. "Like the sheriff, I watch TV. I have a cell phone, one that I was given when I went into the witness protection program. On *NCIS*, they track people with cell phones all the time. I was only to use this one for emergencies, to get in touch with Marshal Norville's office."

"They've never used it to get in touch with you?" Cody asked.

"No. In the last six months, I've only ever been contacted by the local office, and they used my regular land line. But after the shooting at the airport, I used it to contact Marshal Norville."

"Let me see it," Cody said.

Swallowing again, Brie pulled it out of her pocket and placed it in Cody's outstretched hand.

It took him less than half a minute to locate the device.

"I'd say that's how our mystery woman tracked you," Nate said.

"I should have thought of it," Cody said. "Maxine should have thought of it. She knows she has a leak in her office. This gadget is probably how they tracked us to Times Square."

"If you've got a plan B, I could get you off the island," Nate offered.

"I may take you up on that, but not yet," Cody said. "First, I need to think. Then, we need to make sure we don't have anything else planted on us. I figure mystery woman's untimely death buys us some time. Most pros only report in when a job has been completed."

Nate shifted his gaze to Brie. "I'll try and persuade him to get you away from here if you'd like. Your call."

Brie didn't hesitate for a moment. "I'm fine here with Cody. He hasn't failed me so far. And I intend to take a more proactive role in keeping myself safe."

Nate nodded at her, then shifted his attention back to Cody. "If I were you, I'd fill Avery Cooper in, and I think you can trust Mac Davies, too." He glanced down at his watch. "I'll be back up at the hotel in a couple of hours."

"Thanks, Nate. I appreciate the backup," Cody said as the sheriff headed for his car.

"No problem. I have a room booked. Most everyone in Belle Bay is going to be at that Singles Mixer tonight." He glanced back at them when he reached the door of his car. "One word of advice. I wouldn't go near that fantasy box if I were you. You've got enough trouble on your plate."

# 5

"NICE DIGS," BRIE MURMURED more to herself than Cody as they walked into the lobby of Haworth House.

Cody said nothing, but she could tell by the scowl on his face that he wasn't pleased with the lines in front of the registration desk.

She, on the other hand, was. It bought her some time.

They'd had a disagreement on the ride up to the hotel. It had all started when he'd told her his plan was to tuck her safely away in their room while he talked to Avery and did some research.

She'd voiced her vehement objection to that plan, pointing out that a moving target was harder to hit than a stationary one.

"We'll discuss it further once we get checked in."

She'd bitten her tongue.

Oh, there was a lot she could have said. Like she was through with being a good sport and following orders. Where had that gotten her? If that GPS thingy had been planted on her the whole six months she'd spent in

Kansas, she'd given up her passion of singing and waited tables for nothing. Dicky Ferrante could have gotten rid of her at any time.

And something—perhaps her survival instinct—told her that if Dicky didn't know where she was right now, he would soon.

But basically, Cody knew all of that. And she'd learned a long time ago that rants, while they were emotionally rewarding, weren't her best persuasive tool. She needed to come up with a logical argument. So the longer she could avoid being carted off to the room and dumped, the better.

She risked a sideways glance at him, and her heart did a little flutter thing. Even with a scowl on his handsome face, he made her blood heat and her mouth water. Just looking at him was all it took to rekindle the memory of being pressed against that long, lean body, with that clever mouth covering hers.

She'd forgotten to breathe. Thinking had been off the table, too. Both had been banished by the intensity of the feelings he'd aroused in her.

Her world had narrowed down to those lips moving on hers, whispering against hers. To those hands molding her hips and the back of her head. All she'd been able to think of was having more.

And if he turned to her right now and took her hand, she'd follow him anywhere.

This time her heart did more than flutter. She was pretty sure it actually skipped a beat.

Panic bubbled up and warred with bafflement. What was wrong with her? And who was Cody that he could stir her up like this?

She had serious issues on her plate. And in spite of her be-sensible-and-adult strategy, she was outrageously tempted to shove everything else aside to make room for Cody Marsh.

*Wrong place. Wrong time.* She tried repeating the words in her head like a mantra.

He turned and met her eyes. When his immediately darkened to the color of smoke rising from a raging fire, it was suddenly the right place. An image flashed brightly into her mind. She was wrapped around him, a door at her back, and he was touching her the way he hadn't yet.

The way she wanted him to.

And she was touching him. The way she hungered to.

A giddy mix of shock, anticipation and inevitability rushed through her.

Though she hadn't thought it possible, his eyes grew even hotter. He was thinking about it, too. Of what it would be like when they made love.

The certainty of that made her lose all feeling in her legs. For just an instant, her whole world closed in. She was only certain of one thing. She could lose herself in him.

As fear and her instinct for survival kicked in, she struggled to replace the image in her mind with a bucket of ice water pouring over her head.

"Look." Cody's voice was low. Hoarse. But at least he could talk. She wasn't sure she could.

"I know you don't want to go to the room. But I need to think. There's something nagging at me. Something that's important and I can't quite bring it into focus. You're distracting me."

The problem was mutual, she thought. What had happened to her be-adult-and-sensible strategy?

"As soon as we register, I'm going to have Avery take

you up to the room. If I take you, we won't even make it to the bed."

Bed...

Brie pulled up the image of yet another bucket of ice water—this one bigger and colder than the first. Finally, she was able to drag her gaze away from Cody and focus on her surroundings. Lucky for her, the airy lobby of Haworth House had a lot to look at.

She stared first at the intricately carved ceiling, then shifted to the honey-colored parquet floors. A wide staircase swept upward to a landing before splitting at right angles to ascend to the second floor. Through an open archway, she spotted a sunny courtyard where people sat and ate at tables.

"Is it always this busy?" Good. She could talk, and her voice sounded almost normal. Not only were there three lines in front of the registration desk, but all of the seats in the spacious lobby were filled.

"No."

His tone was flat. And tense.

She swept her gaze around the room again. Had he sensed something? Or someone? But everyone she saw looked like...tourists simply enjoying the ambience of the hotel.

Even the people lined up at the registration desk looked perfectly normal.

Brie gave the room another quick scan. None of the hairs on the back of her neck had snapped to attention—not the way they usually did just before her fight or flight response kicked in.

She shifted her gaze back to a tall, ridiculously handsome man behind the registration desk. He had dark skin, the build of a linebacker and he seemed to be in charge of checking guests in.

She glanced at her watch. Clearly, they weren't getting into their room any time soon, so she'd best take advantage of the time. If she could just show Cody that he needed her. She knew how to handle men, she reminded herself. A woman who made her living singing in night clubs and bars didn't last long if she didn't learn how to handle the male of the species.

She pitched her voice low so that only Cody could hear. "I understand you need to think, but I can help you. Two heads are better than one. And I can read people fairly well. For example, from the look on your face, I can tell what you're thinking right now."

He flicked her a glance. "Enlighten me."

"You'd like to bully your way to the front of the line. But that would cause a scene and get us noticed. So you're not going to do it."

"Correct."

"And it might seriously annoy the guy with the megawatt smile who looks like he just posed for *GQ*. I'm assuming that's Avery Cooper, the manager."

Relief rippled through her when the corners of his mouth twitched. "Correct, again."

"Well. I can see why Sheriff Kirby told you to talk to him. He looks as though he could provide some seriously helpful backup if we encounter another problem."

"That's just it." The tension was back in his voice. "We weren't supposed to run into any problems. I was hoping by bringing you here, I wouldn't need backup."

She gave a little laugh. "Except from a ghost."

"I'm still counting on her." He glanced around. "I need a quiet place to think and to use my laptop."

"I think we have to find out who in the marshal's office is on Dicky's payroll."

He met her eyes. "You're right. But you don't have

to worry about any of that. Once I get you to our room, you're staying put until I come up with a plan B. It shouldn't take me long."

Brie opened her mouth to argue but clamped it closed again when another voice spoke.

"Mr. Marsh?"

They both turned to see a young woman with red hair, wearing the khaki slacks and shirt that identified staff members. Her name tag read Tess.

"I remember you from your last visit. Mr. Cooper asked me to keep an eye out for you and your fiancée. While you're waiting to check in, the hotel would like to offer you a complimentary lunch out in the courtyard. If you'd just follow me?"

Sensing that Cody was about to refuse, Brie beamed a smile at Tess. "You're a life saver. I'm starved, but I have an allergy to the sun. Could we eat in the bar instead?"

"Technically, it's not open yet. But I can seat you and take your order. Right this way."

"It will be much more private than the courtyard." Brie spoke in a hushed voice so that only Cody would hear. "At this time of day, it's probably deserted. And I really am starved. While we eat, you can ask Tess to give a message to Avery so that he can join us. That way, we can fill him in and perhaps we can skip the registra—"

She broke off the instant she stepped into the shadowy bar. "Ohh."

"It's quite stunning, isn't it?" Tess asked.

Like everything else Brie had seen so far, the room radiated both tradition and charm. On the far wall, windows framed formal gardens. But the real eye-catcher was the U-shaped bar, a fluid curve of rich mahogany and gleaming brass that stood at the center of the room and provided a free flow of traffic. Guests could choose to sit at the bar, at intimate tables, or in booths.

"It's perfect." In terms of class and style, the place was a far right turn from the bars where she'd paid a lot of her dues. Sometime, she promised herself, she'd sing in a place like this. But it wasn't until she glanced into the shadowy corner to her right that she saw it.

"The piano." Grabbing Cody's arm, she pulled him toward it.

It sat on a small raised stage. Mirrors glittered behind it, a parquet dance floor circled it, and a darkened, crystal chandelier hung overhead.

"Not just any piano," she breathed. "It's a grand. And I think it's a Steinway."

"You're right, ma'am," Tess said. "Ms. Haworth, the original owner, had it built."

When she was close enough, Brie reached out and ran her free hand along the shiny wood. "It's tuned?"

"Absolutely," Tess said. "We have live music every weekend."

"And someone gets to play it?" Brie asked.

"The Brightman sisters believe that's what Hattie would have wanted. Where would you like to sit?"

*Right on top of that piano,* Brie thought. With every fiber of her being, she wanted to climb up on that stage, onto the piano and croon the first few bars of "Someone to Watch Over Me."

"Over there," Cody said.

Out of the corner of her eye, Brie saw him gesture to Tess. And she felt the tug on her arm.

"Brie?"

"Give me just a minute."

He did. In the background, she was aware that he

ordered food. She also caught Avery's name and sensed Tess's departure. But she couldn't drag her gaze away from the piano.

She knew she was taking more than a minute. Just as she was about to turn, she caught something in the mirror. An image of a woman in a long white dress with golden curls tumbling to her shoulders. She was seated on the grand piano, her legs crossed. And she was singing.

Not the song that had been in Brie's head seconds ago, but the one she always ended her performances with. "When You Wish Upon a Star."

"Brie?"

At the sound of Cody's voice, both the image and the music vanished. She blinked and narrowed her eyes.

Nothing.

As she turned and followed Cody to a booth, she gave her head a little shake to clear it. She'd never been a fanciful woman, she reminded herself. She wasn't one to let her imagination run wild. The simple explanation was that she was tired—after all, someone had tried to kill her three times in less than the same number of days—and she was starved. When was the last time she'd eaten?

Food. That's what she should be thinking of. That and convincing Cody not to stuff her away in a room.

Still, she glanced over her shoulder as they reached the booth.

Nothing.

It was that one last backward look that had her sliding into the booth and smack into Cody. Suddenly, they were face to face, shoulder to shoulder, thigh to thigh. Her throat went dry and the air grew very thick. So thick she couldn't get a breath.

Neither one of them moved. She wasn't sure she could, not when her blood had begun to simmer and her bones to melt. His face was so strong—all those sharp angles and lean planes. The glorious hair—overlong and tipped with gold. Just looking at it had her fingers itching to touch the strands. And as if all of that wasn't enough, there were his compelling eyes. This close she could see the color darken, see herself trapped in that deepening gray. Her heart bounced hard and high.

"Shit," he breathed. "I have to kiss you again."

*Couldn'ts* and *shouldn'ts* danced at the corners of her mind, warning of disaster. But the desire, the need grew so intense, so…necessary. "Yeah."

Eyes open, they both moved until their mouths met and melded. She should have known what to expect. She should have been prepared. But once again, a response was ripped out of her before she could prevent it. She felt wild and wanton and wonderful. Her tongue tangled aggressively with his, taking, demanding.

In a sudden move, he shifted, and his hard, rangy body pressed her into the back of the booth. His hands slid up her torso, pressing against the sides of her breasts, then cupping them. She arched closer and allowed herself to do what she hadn't before. She shoved her fingers through that glorious hair.

Sensations rioted through her, blocking out thought. There was nothing but him—his arms, his lips, those sleek, hard muscles.

When they broke apart, it was only to breathe. The sound filled her ears. The air burned her lungs.

"Again," he said.

"Yes." She fisted her hands in his hair and dragged his mouth back to hers.

Once again, she flooded his senses until reality faded

and there was nothing, no one but her. Her mouth was like sin, the silken texture of her skin like heaven. And she made him want her with a wildness and a desperation that he'd never experienced before.

Because he simply couldn't help himself, he ran his hands over her again, absorbing the subtle, almost fragile curves. The tremor that moved through her thrilled him. The moan had him desperate for more. He wanted—no, he needed—flesh to flesh contact. He had to have her beneath him, those strong, slim legs wrapped around him. And then, finally, he would lose himself in her.

*Lose himself.*

It was only as those two words penetrated that Cody was able to pull back and get a thin, tenuous grip on reality again.

They were in a booth. In a public bar. And someone was trying to kill her. With his pulse pounding and needs still clawing through his gut, he managed to release her and put some distance between them.

Would he be able to keep his distance?

That was the number one question in his mind as he watched her open heavy eyes and flick her tongue over her lips as if she wanted to absorb the last hint of his flavor. That simple reaction on her part might have negated all his good intentions if Tess hadn't appeared just then with their food.

After setting three plates on the table, she said, "What else can I get for you?"

"Not a thing," Cody said. "We're fine."

"We're not fine," Brie whispered the moment Tess was out of earshot. "We're crazy. We almost…"

"Yes, we did," Cody agreed. He pushed two of the plates toward her. "I ordered you a cheeseburger and fries and a spinach salad. I wasn't sure what you liked."

"The burger's great." She met his eyes over the top of it. "I'm only letting you distract me with food because I'm starved. But we have to talk about this and—"

She nearly dropped the sandwich. "You made me almost forget."

He bit into a fry. "What?"

"What does this Hattie Haworth look like?"

He met her eyes immediately. "They say she has long golden curls and wears a white dress that floats around her. Why?"

Brie set her sandwich down on the plate. "I think I just saw her."

# 6

"WHERE? TELL ME THE DETAILS," Cody said.

"I just caught a glimpse of her." Brie picked up a fry and pointed in the direction of the piano. "She was sitting on the Steinway in a typical chanteuse position."

Cody looked over his shoulder, then met Brie's eyes again. "Chanteuse position?"

"Legs crossed, leaning back on her hands. Think Michelle Pfeiffer in *The Fabulous Baker Boys*. I could demonstrate."

"I've got it. Think low profile."

"Another time then." She bit into her burger and spoke around the first bite. "You didn't see her?"

"No. When exactly did she appear?"

"You were talking to Tess about the food. I couldn't seem to take my eyes off the piano."

"I noticed."

"It was just as I was about to turn away that I saw her. And I heard her, too."

Cody leaned forward. "What did she say?"

"She sang."

"A song?"

Brie nodded as she took another bite of burger and

chewed. "But it wasn't the song that had been in my head when I'd imagined myself sitting on the piano. And it wasn't my voice. Hers is deeper. Throatier. But it was the song that I end every performance with. It's sort of my signature. 'When You Wish Upon a Star.'"

"Hattie doesn't appear to everyone. I've seen her lover, but not her yet. And as far as I know, she hasn't spoken or sung to anyone before."

She salted her fries. "You're the one with the talent for seeing ghosts. Why do you suppose she appeared to me and not to you?"

"It's an interesting question—but I'll bet the answer lies with Hattie."

"There's a part of me that wants to believe she was a figment of my imagination. But I know what I saw. In a way, it's like that night when I stepped out into the alley and saw that scumbag murder my boss. Once I got far enough away, I wanted to deny what I'd seen. To convince myself that I'd imagined it all. But I knew what I'd seen that time, too."

"Telling the police was a brave thing to do," Cody said.

"No. It was a practical decision. Dicky saw me. He even took a shot at me. It wasn't going to take him long to find out who I was. I needed protection."

Cody reached for her hand and squeezed it. Instantly, he felt the same connection that he'd felt twice before. "I'm going to protect you, Brie."

"And I can increase your chances of doing that."

He opened his mouth, but she held up a finger. "Let me finish."

"Go ahead."

She met his eyes steadily. "I already gave you the whole two heads are better than one spiel."

"I usually work by myself."

"Same here. Much less hassle." She tilted her head to the side and studied him. "Have you ever seen the Steven Segal movie, *Under Siege?*"

"He's a Navy SEAL/cook on a war ship that's hijacked by Tommy Lee Jones and buddies?"

She pointed a fry at him. "That's the one. I feel just like Miss January—the girl who popped out of the cake at the captain's birthday party. You've saved my life twice, so I figure the safest place for me is with you. That's how she convinced Steven Segal not to stuff her away in a locker. And later on in that movie, she saves his life. I think we're better off as a team."

She had a point. Besides, there was something in her eyes, something he hadn't seen before. Vulnerability. She hid it well. Perhaps that was why it pulled at him. "Okay. We'll stick together."

"Thanks." She smiled, and he felt the warmth shoot straight to his center.

Then she dropped her gaze to one of the platters. "Do you want any more fries?"

He pushed the plate toward her. "Are you going to eat any of that salad?"

She wrinkled her nose as she swirled a fry in ketchup. "Do I look like Popeye?"

He laughed as he pulled the salad toward him. "You don't look like Olive Oyl, either."

"I hope not." She swallowed a fry. "Why the CIA?"

Cody speared some spinach. "I went to law school to please my parents. But after one year at my grandfather's firm, I was bored to tears. The only thing I liked about being an attorney was the research—trying to discover the solution to a problem. Going to court and actually arguing the case was tedious. So it wasn't too tough for my friend, Ian MacFarland, to recruit me. He's engaged to one of the Brightman sisters now, but back then he worked as an analyst for the CIA."

She tilted her head to one side. "Why'd you leave?"

"Bored again. I enjoyed the research and analysis, but I couldn't follow through on it. I handed it over to someone else who acted on it—or not. Plus, I discovered I didn't like working for other people."

"I guess your current career choice doesn't get boring."

He laughed. "You're right. Although I haven't had many days like today. How about you? How'd you get to be a singer?"

"I always wanted to be one. Ever since I can remember, I've had songs in my head."

"Did your mother sing to you?"

"I like to think so, but I was adopted when I was two so I can't be sure if she actually did—or if I just fantasize that she did."

"You never once had a doubt, never wavered about a singing career?"

"Never." She met his eyes. "And I'm not going to waver now."

"There they are."

The voice had Brie turning toward the archway that opened into the lobby. Tess was hurrying toward them, followed by a tall woman and an even taller man. The woman was carrying what looked like a hat box.

"Cody?" It was the woman who spoke, and when she reached their booth, Cody slid out to give her a quick hug.

"Good to see you, Reese," Cody said.

"We've been looking all over for you. Mac and I were

on our way to meet someone and we ran into Avery and Nate in the lobby. Both were concerned that you hadn't checked in yet. We split up to find you."

"I'll let the others know where you are," Tess said before hurrying off.

"Brie, I'd like you to meet Reese Brightman."

"And I'm Mac Davies," the man said.

Reese set her hat box down on a nearby table. "Nate filled us in *very* briefly on what happened to you on the way up here."

"What can we do to help?" Mac asked.

"Keep your eyes open," Cody said. "And as far as everyone else is concerned, Brie is my fiancée and we're here on a little getaway. What you might find interesting is that Brie has already had an encounter with Hattie. I'll let her tell you about it."

Both Mac and Reese shifted their gazes to her.

"I think I saw her on the piano, and she was singing," Brie said.

Reese exchanged a look with Mac. "Hattie's had a busy day. This morning, she and Samuel were out on the cliffs saving my life. No one who's seen her has ever mentioned her speaking before. What did she sing to you, Brie?"

They were all looking at her again. No one had a doubt that she'd actually seen a ghost. And heard one.

"'When You Wish Upon a Star.' The odd thing is that it's a song I always sing at the end of my performances. And it's not part of the standard repertoire of night club singers."

"No," Mac said. "It's from Disney's *Pinocchio*. I remember my mother used to sing it to me when I was little. How long have you been singing?"

"All my life," Brie said. "Just before I saw Hattie, I

was imagining myself on that piano. None of my gigs so far have offered a Steinway. But the more I think about it, the more I'm wondering if I just imagined it. Or her."

Reese reached for her hand and gave it a squeeze. "I know the feeling. I felt exactly that way the first time I saw her in the mirror in the tower room. I didn't want to believe that she might be real. But she is." She glanced at Mac again. "And I'm very grateful to her."

Brie was aware that Cody had shifted slightly in front of her before she saw that Nate and Avery Cooper were nearly upon them.

"You two are tough to track down," Nate said.

"That's our goal," Cody said.

"You must be Brie," Avery said, and she found herself enveloped in a warm hug. "Welcome to Haworth House." Keeping his hands on her shoulders, he stepped back. "I'm sorry that your ride up here was a bit rough and even sorrier we were so busy when you arrived. If I can do anything to make it up to you, just say the word."

Perhaps if his voice hadn't sounded so sincere, or perhaps if the piano hadn't been in her line of vision… or perhaps if she hadn't had a momentary flashback of seeing Hattie sitting there, legs crossed, smiling at her, she might have been able to stop herself.…

Because the idea was both reckless and dangerous. And wonderful. In the end, the words just popped out. "I want to sing on that piano."

"Done," Avery said.

"No." Cody and Nate spoke in unison.

"It's too dangerous. I've got information on our mystery woman," Nate said. "Her name is Marielle Radtke, and she's in the major leagues when it comes to hit men for hire. She works with a partner. Interpol has a huge file on her. Their best theory on the partner is that he's male."

Cody turned to Brie. "Radtke was alone on that motorcycle when she drove onto the ferry. But that doesn't mean her partner didn't get here another way while she was putting on a show. So Radtke's partner could still be on the island—even in this hotel. There's no way you're going to sing in public until after the trial. You might as well paint a target on your back."

Any possible response Brie would have made was postponed when a small brunette rushed into the bar. "Reese, there you are."

The pretty young woman's forward propulsion was halted abruptly when everyone turned to face her.

"Molly." It was Nate who spoke first.

"Nate." After a brief instant of hesitation, the brunette smiled and moved forward. "I'm here to meet with Reese."

"That she is," Reese said. "If you gentleman will excuse us, we'll just move to the other side of the bar for some girl talk." She turned to Brie. "Please join us."

"Yes," Molly said. "I could use the moral support. I'm about to take a very big step."

For one second, maybe less, Brie hesitated, torn. Girl talk was something she hadn't had very much of since college. But she didn't want to leave Cody, didn't want to miss what else Nate might have discovered.

Cody squeezed her hand. "Go ahead. I'll fill you in."

And she could have sworn that Avery winked at her before she turned to follow Reese and Molly.

CODY'S MIND WAS RACING as they all took seats at the far end of the bar. There was something—just at the edge of his mind that was still trying to get his attention. It had been bothering him ever since they'd left the scene of the accident.

He'd spoken nothing but the truth to Brie. He needed time to think. Then it would come. He and Nate had selected seats which offered a clear view of the women. While Avery brewed coffee, Cody tried to marshal his thoughts. If he wasn't going to get alone time, it might help to share his ideas aloud.

"Marielle Radtke," he mused. "That kind of fire power isn't something Ferrante would have easy access to," he said. "I can see him hiring the two goons who tried to gun Brie down at the Kansas City airport and whoever shot at us in Times Square. But a dynamic duo like Radtke and her partner is a little out of his league."

"You're thinking he had help," Nate said.

"Yes." Cody narrowed his eyes on Nate as a thought occurred to him. "You got the information on Radke and partner pretty quickly. I'm thinking you must have contacted Ian or Dane."

"Ian," Nate admitted. "Reese talked to both of her sisters this morning after her near miss. They expect to arrive with Ian and Dane sometime tomorrow. Once I got back to the office, I gave Ian a call. It didn't take him long once I sent him our mystery woman's fingerprints and a photo."

Nate glanced at Mac. "Reese's older sisters are engaged to two brothers who run a top-notch investigation firm."

Mac nodded. "So I've recently learned. MacFarland Investigations. The name rings a bell, but I haven't quite placed it yet."

"They're very good at what they do." Nate turned back to Cody. "Any idea on who might have put Ferrante in touch with Radtke?"

"Yeah. And I don't like it," Cody said. "I'm thinking whoever is behind this latest attempt on Brie's life is going all out to protect his or her ass. If Radtke had succeeded in running us off the cliff, it might have passed as an accident."

Nate's brows shot up. "You think I would have overlooked the fresh cuts on the guardrail cables?"

Cody's smile was thin. "Radtke didn't know you. She thought she was dealing with—"

"A small town hick sheriff," Nate finished.

"Exactly," Cody said as Avery set mugs down.

A giggle had the four men all turning toward the booth where the ladies were seated. Reese had taken the lid off the hat box.

"What's that about?" Nate asked with a frown.

"Molly asked Reese for a favor," Mac explained. "She wants to get a head start and draw out her fantasy now instead of waiting until the big mixer tonight."

"It's all nonsense," Nate muttered.

Cody noted that the sheriff's scowl belied his words.

Curiouser and curiouser. Cody shifted his attention to Molly who had her hands hovering over the hat box. "So that's the famous fantasy box."

"The one and only," Avery said with a sideways glance at Nate. "Its magic goes far beyond fulfilling fantasies. So far Hattie's linen hat box is three for three in the matchmaking department."

"Wish me luck." Molly's voice carried to them.

Nate shifted on his stool so that his back was to the booth. "We have more important things to talk about."

Indeed they did, Cody thought.

# 7

"WISH ME LUCK," MOLLY said. Her hands shook as she extended them over the open hat box. At the last minute, she snatched them back and fisted them on the table in front of her. "He isn't even looking."

"Who?" Brie asked.

"Nate." Reese spoke in a low voice. "He's Molly's first love, and she hasn't gotten over him yet."

"Well, he's gotten over me," Molly said. "I've been back on the island for more than a year, and I might as well be a stranger for all he's noticed me."

Then she leaned close to Brie and pitched her voice low. "Nate was my high school sweetheart, and he dumped me at the senior prom."

"I'm sorry," Brie said.

"In a way, it was the best thing that ever happened to me. I left the island and went to the Fashion Institute in New York City."

"She's really good," Reese put in.

"I thought I'd gotten over Nate Kirby, that I'd washed him out of my hair and out of my heart," Molly continued. "Four years in the Big Apple gave me a new goal—to design clothes for celebs on the red carpet.

But when my grandmother became ill a little over a year ago, I came back to take over her general store."

"And Molly's turned it into a great boutique," Reese said. "She designs most of the clothes, and she's starting to attract buyers from New York."

"Yeah." Molly sighed. "The only problem is I haven't gotten over Nate, and he's not interested." She shot a glare at Nate's back. "This is do or die for me. I'm moving on."

"I think I met your grandmother on the ferry coming over. Her name's Clarissa, right?"

"That's her," Molly said. "She's retired now, but she's running my store this weekend so I can do this."

"You just have to be sure you want to do it." Reese tipped up the lid off the box and pointed to the warning.

Brie leaned closer to read it: *The fantasy you draw out will come true.* "Your grandmother talked about the fantasies. Is this warning for real?" she asked Molly.

"Absolutely," Reese added. "My sisters and I can all testify to that. The fantasies we pulled out all came true. For Naomi and Jillian, it was a forbidden fantasy they'd each secretly entertained in their early teens. And Hattie not only fulfilled those fantasies, she hooked them up with Dane and Ian MacFarland."

"Cody mentioned Ian," Brie said.

"They were in the CIA together," Reese said. "The MacFarlands have had a rough time of it. Their mother died when they were just kids and the whole family was split up. Ian and his younger brother and sister were adopted. Dane got shuffled around in the foster care system. He finally tracked Ian down about a year ago, and the two of them are determined to find their other siblings."

"Wait," Molly said. "Back up a minute. Did I hear you say that your fantasy came true also? You didn't mention that last night when I ran into you in the bar."

Reese smiled and blushed a little. "That's because it hadn't come true yet. And I wasn't so sure it would. I was positive Hattie's fantasy for me was a mistake. I was supposed to experience all the pleasures of having my own boy toy." Reese laughed. "Boy toy? Not my style at all. Until I ran into Mac in the lobby."

At the sound of Reese's laugh, Brie noted that all four men glanced over at their table. Then Nate turned his back to them.

"That's it. I'm doing this," Molly said in a low, determined voice. "I'm moving on. And I'm hoping Hattie's fantasy works as fast for me as it did for you. I'm closing doors to the past, and opening doors to the future."

"You're beginning to sound like a self-help tape," Reese said.

A martial light came to Molly's eyes. "You're right. Been there, tried those." She turned to Brie. "Leaving Belle Island and attending school in New York was the smartest thing I've ever done. Coming back here and opening my own store is the second smartest thing. But this…" She pointed to the fantasy box. "This is going to go to the top of the list."

When she pulled out a parchment envelope from the box, another one floated to the table in front of Brie. But her attention was totally diverted by the changing expressions on Molly's face.

Puzzlement.

"I don't get it," she murmured. "Unless…"

Next came surprise.

"Ohh."

Comprehension dawned on Molly's face.

"I think I get it." As Molly slipped the parchment back into its envelope and into her purse, her expression turned thoughtful.

"Aren't you going to tell us what you drew out?" Brie asked.

Molly shook her head, her expression still very thoughtful. "It might not be what I think it is. And I don't want either of you to tell me I'm wrong. That might pull the plug on my courage."

She slid out of the booth and was halfway to the lobby when she stopped, turned back, and waved. "I'll see you both at the Singles Mixer tonight."

Brie stared at her until she disappeared. "Now my curiosity is really piqued."

"Fantasies are private things. My sisters and I never told each other what we'd drawn out until after our fantasies had come true. I think it's kind of like a wish. There's always that fear that if you give voice to it, it might not come true."

"Like when you blow out your birthday candles and you can't tell anyone what you asked for."

"Exactly." Then Reese glanced down at the envelope lying in front of Brie. "Why don't you open yours?"

"Mine? No. This one just fell out of the box when Molly took hers."

"Hattie doesn't make mistakes where her fantasy box is concerned. Take it from someone who knows. That one is definitely yours."

Brie couldn't seem to take her eyes off the yellowing envelope. The temptation to open it was fierce. But fantasies were dangerous. They made you want things. Then unable to prevent herself, she shifted her gaze to Cody.

The pull was instant and so intense that she nearly

went to him. She'd never wanted anyone the way she wanted Cody Marsh. But it wasn't the time or the place.

The woman who'd tried to kill them only a matter of hours ago had a partner. Someone who could be lurking right now somewhere in the resort, just waiting for the opportune moment.

A song drifted into her mind, one of the saddest songs she ever sang—"Somewhere" from *West Side Story*. The lovers in that play had only found a small window of opportunity to be together. She and Cody were in the same situation.

Perhaps this would be their only time together. If she didn't grab it, she might lose it forever.

She lifted the envelope and pulled out the fantasy. *You will push the past and the future aside to indulge in a onetime fling.*

A band tightened around her heart as she reread the writing on the parchment paper.

"Don't worry if it doesn't seem to fit," Reese said. "I thought Hattie had made a mistake with me, too."

"No, it fits." She raised her eyes, and the instant she did, her gaze locked with Cody's. Even at this distance, she could feel the heat of those gray eyes. "Perfectly."

It was the perfect fantasy. The only one she could ever have with Cody.

And she intended to indulge in it. Fully.

"WHAT DO YOU SAY?"

Cody dragged his eyes away from Brie's. Every time he looked at her, he lost his train of thought. He had to put a stop to that. He was almost sure that it was Mac who'd spoken to him. "Sorry?"

"I was just saying that if Nate really feels you should

leave, I can help. If you can give me until tomorrow morning, I can have a private jet waiting for you in Portland. I'll have my pilot arrange for a helicopter to transport you there."

"Have you still got Brie's phone?" Nate asked.

Cody fished it out of his pocket.

"I can arrange for it to go back to the mainland on the morning ferry."

"A little misdirection," Cody mused. "The thing is, I'm not sure it would work. If Radtke's partner is still here, as we suspect, he or she might have spotted us already." He paused for a second as something once more pushed at the edge of his mind.

"All the more reason to get you off the island," Nate said.

"I just don't trust that we won't be tracked or followed." Cody ran his hands through his hair. "So far they've been one step ahead of me all the way. Someone in the Federal Marshal's office is on Ferrante's payroll. That was why Maxine Norville called me in. And it's someone high enough up that they would know how to contact and hire Marielle Radtke and her partner."

"Go on," Nate prompted.

"I figure this person has as much to lose as Ferrante at this point. If Brie testifies and sends Ferrante to death row, he's going to make a deal and sing, pardon the cliché, like a canary. So it's not just his brother and grandfather and other business associates who have a stake in silencing Brie."

Mac held up a hand. "You're saying someone in the marshal's office is also out to kill her?"

"That's the way I see it," Cody said. "If I'm right, the moment I turn her over to testify on Monday, I've signed her death warrant."

Silence fell for three beats. It was Nate who finally broke it. "So what do we do?"

"It we can draw out Radtke's partner and capture him, we may get him/her to flip on who's picking up the tab for their services."

"How could we do that without putting Brie in danger?" Mac asked.

"We couldn't," Cody said. "The trick will be to minimize the danger." His gaze was drawn to the piano.

Mac turned to Avery. "These MacFarland brothers—they're supposed to be good. Can't they create another identity for Brie and get her out of this death trap?"

Cody glanced at Mac. "They could. But that means Ferrante walks and so does his bosom buddy in the Federal Marshal's office. Plus, Brie wants to sing again. And she might just be good enough to make a name for herself. If she does, someone's going to be able to trace her."

"But how do we draw out Radtke's partner without getting Brie killed?" Nate asked.

There were a few beats of silence. Cody found his gaze shifting to the piano again. Something shimmered in the mirror. And then he saw Hattie, just as Brie had described her. She was sitting on the piano, legs crossed and leaning back on her hands. She winked at him before she faded.

At that instant, the thing that had been nagging at him all day clicked into focus.

"The timing," he murmured.

The other three men fixed their attention on him.

"Something's been bothering me ever since Brie and I left the accident scene. I don't doubt that the GPS tracking device in Brie's phone was how Radtke tracked us.

But she needed time to cut the guardrail cables. And I think I know how she got it."

"We're all ears," Nate said.

"There was a stalled car in the intersection on Main Street right in front of the coffee shop. The only person who got past it was Radtke on her bike. Brie and I, as well as several other people, were stuck there for nearly half an hour. I think the driver had to be Radtke's partner. His job was to keep us there until she could get the cables cut. The guy was none too happy when I insisted that he get out of his car and help us push it off to a side street."

"You got a good look at him, I presume," Nate said.

"Gray hair, thick glasses."

"He could have been wearing a disguise," Nate added.

"I agree. But he can't disguise his height or build. He was very tall and skinny, like Ichabod Crane from *The Legend of Sleepy Hollow.*"

Nate pulled out his phone. "I'll call my deputy Tim and have him put the word out."

"I'll alert the staff," Avery said.

When he'd finished on his phone, Nate narrowed his eyes on Cody. "You're thinking of setting a trap."

"The way I see it, I've already led Brie into one. I just want to spring it on a different person."

"We could lose her," Nate said.

Cody met his eyes. "I stand to lose her anyway come Monday."

Nate sighed. "What's the plan?"

Cody glanced at the piano again. Hattie wasn't there this time, but she'd succeeded in planting the idea. He was going to believe she would back them up. "Brie's going to sing here tonight."

"It's too dangerous," Nate said.

"It's the best chance we've got of drawing the guy out. There are four of us," Cody said. "We can cover both exits. If she's sitting on that piano, the guy won't be able to get a clear shot from either the lobby or the gardens. He'll have to come into the bar. We know what he looks like and we have the advantage of picking the time and the place." He turned to Avery, "What time does the Singles Mixer start?"

"Nine o'clock."

"Then a good time for Brie to sing would be around ten or ten-thirty."

"Perfect. And we'll have more than four men, actually," Avery said. "Colonel Jenkins is registered." He turned to Mac. "You haven't met him yet, but he's a retired military man and related to Hattie Haworth's lover. I'm sure he'd agree to help. He's going to be at the mixer tonight, anyway. And then there's Hattie."

When they all turned to stare at him, Avery simply shrugged. "Hey, the lady's three for three in the catching the bad guys and protecting the good guys department. And she seems to like Brie. No one's ever seen her on that piano before. Or heard her sing."

"I need to talk to Brie before we finalize everything," Cody said.

"I've got the perfect spot," Avery said. "Until this matter is resolved, you're going to the tower room. Hattie will take care of you there."

# 8

*Late Friday afternoon—Singles Weekend, Day 1*

As AVERY LED THE WAY UP a narrow stone stairway to the tower floors, Brie was very much aware of Cody following behind her and of the parchment envelope she still held tightly in her hand. Before they'd left the bar, Cody had informed her of his theory about the man in the stalled car being Marielle Radtke's partner. It made sense.

At the top of the stairs, Avery turned down a short corridor. "The sisters keep a suite of rooms on this level." He indicated a door as they passed it. But he didn't stop until they reached a large, ornately carved oak door at the end of the hall.

"There's no key," Avery explained as he punched numbers into a keypad. "MacFarland Investigations set up the security, and not even the staff has the code. You'll be perfectly safe."

When the door swung open, Brie stepped into a small space that's sole function was to house a circular iron staircase that wound upward. All the light came from either above or the hall behind them.

"If there's anything you want, use the room phone to contact me," Avery said.

The door swung shut with a solid click that seemed to fill the small space.

All Brie wanted was the man standing right beside her. For a moment, the silence stretched between them. She moistened her lips.

It wasn't that she was having second thoughts. It was just that this was new for her. Oh, she took risks, all right. You couldn't be faint of heart and embark on a singing career.

But those risks had been professional, and she'd always had a fall-back plan. Caution had always been the number one rule in her personal life. And she had no fall-back plan with Cody. There was only this time. This place.

She tightened her grip on the parchment as she turned to him. His face was shadowed in the filtered sunlight that fell from the room above, but she could see his eyes. And what she saw was exactly what she wanted.

She took a step forward.

He did the same.

They were almost touching.

"There's something I need to talk to you about, and then you need to rest," he said.

"Later," she said. "Right now, let's pretend."

"Pretend?"

"Yeah. Let's imagine that no one is trying to kill me." She took another step forward. "For now, there's only me and you. Nothing else exists."

"That's the problem. When I'm with you, nothing else does." He set down the backpack and the duffel. Then he lifted his hands, pulled the fastener off of her pony tail and threaded his fingers through her hair. "I promised myself that I wasn't going to do this." He skimmed his hands over her shoulders and down her arms.

"What you said was we'd never make it to the bed," she reminded him.

"Yeah." Settling his hands at her waist, he drew her so close to him that she could feel every line and angle.

Brie linked her arms around his neck and drew his mouth down to hers. Then rising up on her toes so that she could close that last little distance, she said, "Show me what else you promised yourself not to do."

"How about this?" His mouth brushed over hers—once, twice—tasting, teasing, testing. He hadn't kissed her like this before, as if he had endless time and intended to take it.

Fast was what she'd had in mind. That was what she'd anticipated. But the way his teeth nibbled on her lip, the way his tongue licked at the corner of her mouth—how could she have known she needed this?

His tongue toyed with hers, tangling, then sliding away as layer after layer of delicious pleasure built. Time—the precious amount that they had—seemed to spin away as they stood in the stairwell of the tower and dust motes danced around them.

She wasn't even aware of just when the rhythm of the kiss changed—only that it had. Warmth blossomed into heat. When his teeth sank into her bottom lip, fire shot to her toes. His flavors were darker now, richer, the movement of his mouth on hers faster. Not patient any longer, but desperate. With lips, tongue and teeth, he drove her to the edge of reason until he drew everything from her.

Everything.

And he kept on taking. Her heart had never beat this fast. She was sure of it. Until Cody, her body had never ached and pulsed like this. She'd never dreamed it could. Now, she wanted more. What else could he show her?

And she wanted him to show her now. Right now.

She wasn't sure if she'd said the words or merely thought them, but he spun her against the door and took his hands on a desperate, meticulous journey from her throat to her breasts, then down her torso to her waist. She dug her fingers into his shoulders, scooted up and locked her legs around him.

For one glorious moment, they were center to center, heat to heat. But it wasn't enough.

She was driving him crazy. The pressure of that slim body locked around his drove him to the edge of reason. That was all Cody could think as he turned and braced his back against the wall. Her hips were pumping now, and each movement stoked the fire in his loins that had already reached flash point.

With a groan, he dragged his mouth from hers. "Wait," he said.

"Can't."

And she didn't. She continued to move against him, faster and faster.

"Can't," she said again. "Can't quite…"

Cody was pretty sure he could. And soon. He could feel his own climax starting to build at the base of his spine. "I want to be inside of you."

He wasn't sure he could survive another ten seconds if he wasn't inside of her. He took a stumbling step forward, then dropped to his knees. Even then, it took all of his strength to push her away and settle her on the second step.

With lightning speed, she reached for the snap on his jeans.

"Wait," he said again. "There's something…"

"What?"

He shook his head, trying to clear some portion of it. "Protection...I—"

"Got it covered. I'm on the pill."

"Good."

They attacked her clothes together, pulling at her jeans. She scooted up another step while he dragged the denim down her legs and tugged off her shoes.

"Hurry," she said, grabbing again at the snap of his jeans.

"There's probably a bed upstairs." He managed to get the jeans down his hips.

"Later," she said as she dragged the T-shirt over his head.

"Right." He had to get his hands on her again. This time on her skin. He pulled her T-shirt off, and bracing her against the stair railing, he ran his hands over her—those graceful shoulders, the swell of her breasts and that strong, lean torso. Lifting her up a step, he took his mouth on that same fast journey.

Her taste flooded him—so sweet, so hot. So necessary.

"Now. Right now."

Had he said it? Had she?

All he was sure of was that when he looked into those glorious eyes, he wanted her more than anything.

They moved together, he pulling them torso to torso, she wrapping her legs around him.

Keeping his eyes on hers, he said, "Now. Right now."

Then with one savage movement of his hips, he drove into her. Her slick core clenched around him, drenched him and pulled him even deeper.

For one moment, neither of them moved. He wished

he could stop time. To keep both of them right there, teetering on the brink of pleasure and release. But he had to have more. Lifting her hips, he withdrew, then plunged into her again.

When she cried out, gripping him even more tightly as her climax ripped through her, something inside of him snapped. Holding her close, he lifted her and then drove into her again and again.

Her nails dug into his back as her body moved with his, matching his speed—faster and faster, almost on the edge of violence—until he felt the second climax move through her.

*Mine,* he thought just before his own release shattered him.

When reality finally trickled in, Cody's heart was still pumping fast, his breathing was still ragged. And Brie was lying beneath him on the iron stairs.

Cursing himself silently, he rolled, taking her with him, and when he felt the press of the stairs against his own back, he cursed himself again.

"You all right?"

"Mmm."

"I'll bet I left marks on your back."

She raised her head, met his eyes. "If you did, they're worth it."

He laughed, and just that slight ripple of movement through his body had her core tightening around him. He saw first shock and then pleasure move through her as she climaxed again.

Even as he gripped her hips, she braced both hands on his shoulders and smiled down at him. "Let me see if I can return the favor."

Then she began to ride him, slowly at first. But the heat snaked through him, hardening him inside of her.

And then they were racing again, faster and faster, driving each other higher and higher, until she shattered with him again.

CODY TRIED TO PACE OFF his nerves while he waited for Brie to finish primping in the bathroom. His plan to use her as bait to trap a killer was a go, and the clock was ticking on putting that plan into action.

No time for second thoughts, he lectured himself. Especially when he didn't have an alternative.

It had been a while before he and Brie had made it up the stairs to the tower room, before they'd showered and made love again, before he'd told her about the trap he wanted to set that night.

"I'll do it," she'd said.

Just like that. Not a second of hesitation.

He'd known she would agree, and he knew that as dangerous as it was, it was the best chance they had of saving her life.

Still, the instant the words were out of her mouth, fear had gripped his stomach like a rusty claw, and he'd wanted nothing more than to talk her out of it.

"You're sure?" he'd asked.

"Positive. I'm getting pretty tired of playing the sitting duck. Besides, since this guy looks like Ichabod Crane, he ought to be pretty easy to spot."

"Yeah." That was the theory.

"And there'll be a lot of people on the lookout. Avery will alert the staff. Reese will let Molly know. Mac Davies has a good eye—he's a producer. Nate will be around, and we even have a retired army colonel on our side."

"The piano is positioned so that there's no clear way to take a shot at it from the outside garden or the lobby.

Our guy will have to come into the bar." When he'd realized that he was talking more to convince himself than her, he'd shut up.

She'd beamed a smile at him. "Then we'll get him."

That sure as hell was the plan. But after he'd finally convinced her to take a nap on the sofa, he'd divided his time between setting the plan in motion with Nate and Avery and trying to think up a safer alternative.

He'd been successful with the former, but not with the latter.

Stuffing his hands in his pockets, Cody circled around the partial wall that divided the tower room into two spaces. One offered a comfortable sitting room with a fireplace, and the other provided a work area with a breathtaking view of the sea.

The clock was ticking, the plan was in motion. And it would work.

Avery had already put up a sign outside the bar to advertise Brie's performance and the time, 10:00 p.m. About twenty minutes ago, Reese and Mac had tapped lightly on the tower room door to deliver a dress for Brie to wear.

She was getting into it now.

Cody rubbed the back of his neck and sighed. There was something still pushing at the edge of his mind, something that he couldn't quite get a hold of. He knew from experience that it would come to him, just as the possible significance of that stalled car had.

And the best way to facilitate that was to think of something else. With a glance at the bathroom door, he pulled a parchment envelope out of his pocket. He'd found it lying on the floor when he'd gone down to take the dress from Mac and Reese, and the temptation to open it had been gnawing at him ever since.

He'd learned all about Hattie's special hat box and the power it seemed to wield on his first visit to the island when Ian had asked for his help. Later he'd learned that all three sisters had drawn parchments out of Hattie's fantasy box on their very first visit to the tower room. The two older Brightman sisters had not only drawn out fantasies that they'd secretly dreamed about in their teens, but they'd each lived out the fantasy with the man they'd also fallen in love with.

Though he hadn't gotten all the details yet about Reese and Mac, it looked as though they'd also been brought together by one of Hattie's parchments. He couldn't help but be curious about what fantasy Brie had chosen. Turning the envelope over, he pulled it out.

*You will push the past and the future aside to indulge in a onetime fling.*

Something stabbed at his heart as he read the last three words again.

*A onetime fling.*

Was that the fantasy that Brie had carried secretly in her heart?

It made a lot of sense, he thought. She was a woman who'd focused on her career and was now focused on survival.

Well, he'd just have to change her mind. Because he intended to have much more than a onetime fling with Brie Sullivan. He slipped the parchment back into the envelope and set it on a nearby table.

WITH A CRITICAL EYE, Brie studied herself in the mirror. The hair was almost right. She'd pulled it back from her face, then let it fall to her shoulders. Now, she tweaked a few strands loose.

Perfect.

The dress was perfect, too. A sheath of black silk, nearly backless with a halter top. She didn't have a lot of curves, but the thin, stretchy silk clung to each and every one.

But it was her face that Brie's eyes returned to again and again as she checked her image. It was different, and although she had an artful hand, she knew that it wasn't the makeup that was responsible for the change. She glowed. And it was all due to Cody Marsh.

Her body was still vibrating with the sensory memories of what they'd done to each other on the stairs and in the shower.

Pressing her hand to her stomach, she closed her eyes and tried to clear her mind. But it was hard.

Oh, she'd sensed on some level that making love to Cody would be special from the first time she'd taken his hand in Times Square. But she hadn't expected, she hadn't anticipated the reality. How could you even imagine something that you'd never experienced before?

Maybe that was the true allure of a onetime fling fantasy—a memory that you never would have had otherwise. And she would have a doozy. She met her own gaze again in the mirror and firmly ignored the tightening around her heart.

It was time for practical, sensible Brie Sullivan to make a reappearance. She had a major gig tonight. That was what she had to concentrate on.

For the first time in six months, she was going to be able to sing. The downside was that someone was probably going to try to kill her.

The upside was that Mac Davies, the "star-maker"

was going to be in her audience. That's what she had to concentrate on.

And Cody—well, she would always have the memory.

Taking a deep breath, she turned and opened the bathroom door.

# 9

"HOW DO I LOOK?" Brie asked as she stepped into the tower room.

The instant he saw her, Cody experienced what it was like to take a bullet to the gut.

She turned in a little circle, not meeting his eyes, and that gave him plenty of time to use his to take in the nape of her neck, the slender back.

And the legs. He really hadn't had time to fully take them in before. They'd worked okay, running, wrapped around him, but he'd never really had a chance to appreciate how long they were. The spiky heels no doubt made a difference, but how did she walk on them?

As she moved farther into the room, her goal seemed to be the beveled mirror.

Good.

Because if she came within grabbing distance, he knew what he wanted to do, even though he wasn't sure the connection between his brain and his muscles was in working order.

"I clean up pretty good, don't I?" She twirled in front of the glass.

He couldn't say a word. Probably a good thing, since if he opened his mouth, his tongue might hang out.

She faced him, the mirror at her back. "Before we go to the bar, there's something I want to say. What happened earlier—making love to you—I've never... it's never been like that for me."

Cody finally found the strength to move until he was standing with her in front of the mirror. Very carefully, he reached out and framed her face with his hands. "It's never been that way for me, either." Standing there, looking into her eyes, he knew he'd never find with anyone else what he'd found with her.

Brie stepped forward. "Whatever happens tonight, whatever comes afterward, I'll always have the memory of what we shared. No one will be able to take it away. I'll treasure it always."

Memory? It took him a second to figure out what she must be talking about. The fantasy. The onetime fling.

There was a tightening around his heart again and the slightest ripple of fear in his stomach. He wanted more than a memory of her. They hadn't talked. There hadn't been time. And he didn't have enough time right now to tell her what was in his heart. Instead, he framed her face with his hands and pressed his mouth softly to hers.

The instant their lips met, melded, he felt the fear smooth away. This, in the midst of the chaos they'd been through in the past day, felt right. There was no punch of lust, no spiral of need, no molten fire pushing through his blood. In place of all of that was a warmth, steady and true.

He didn't understand it. But standing here, kissing her, quite simply felt right. She had to feel it, too. He watched the glorious green of her eyes cloud and darken as he changed the angle of the kiss. And she trembled.

This was so different. That was the one thought that hadn't fuzzed over in Brie's mind. He'd kissed her softly before, but the tenderness was new.

Even as he deepened the kiss, very slowly, there were none of the demands he'd made before. In their place was a request. He was taking her to a new place. And she melted molecule by molecule until her heart, her soul, her dreams, desires, all she was slipped from her to him.

When she'd surrendered everything, there was nothing left but a soft, drowsy warmth.

She'd come home.

Brie had no idea how long they stood there. All she was certain of was that she wanted the moment to go on and on.

It was the phone that brought them both back to reality. Even then, it wasn't until the second ring that they each drew back.

His hands were still on her face when he said, "Hold on to that memory, too, Brie. There are going to be more."

Then he dropped his hands and moved to pick up the phone. "Yes."

He met her eyes. "Yes, Avery, we're all set. We'll be right down."

CODY SCANNED THE CROWDED BAR. A trio currently occupying the stage played something soft and bluesy. Two couples danced on the small parquet floor.

Between the glow of the overhead chandeliers and the light provided by the candles on the tables, he could see everyone. And if the even ratio of men and women at the bar and tables was any indication, Avery's Singles Mixer was achieving its goal.

Brie was safely tucked away in a booth for now with Reese, Molly and another woman who'd been introduced to him as Miss Emmy Lou Pritchard, the town librarian.

The men were in position. Colonel Jenkins, a man Cody had met on his previous visit, was standing near the exit door at the far end of the bar. It opened into a corridor that accessed the gardens and meeting rooms. Jenkins reminded him of Paul Newman in his later movies, and although he had to be in his early sixties, Cody figured the colonel could handle Radtke's partner if the man entered or tried to exit using that door.

No one who came anywhere near fitting the description of Ichabod Crane was in the bar right now. That didn't surprise Cody. The man hadn't evaded capture this long by being careless. And the death of his partner must have made him wary.

The way Cody figured it, Radtke's partner would spend as little time in the bar as he could—just long enough to take out his target.

When the knot in his stomach tightened, Cody firmly ignored it.

Nate had positioned himself at the archway to the lobby. He had his deputy, Tim, stationed behind the reception desk. If their hit man entered the bar from that direction, Nate would have him.

Mac stood at the bar a few feet away from the women, and Avery was circulating among the guests. Cody had chosen a position next to one of the tall potted trees that framed the little stage. His vantage point gave him a good view of all parts of the bar with the exception of the lobby. It also put him within a few feet of Brie once she climbed onto that piano.

He thought he had everything covered. Then again, that's what he'd thought from the moment he'd taken Maxine Norville's call. He'd been so positive he could do the job. But the feeling was still there, nagging at him—he was missing something.

He shifted his gaze back to Brie and put it out of his mind. For now, he needed to focus all his attention on keeping her safe.

REESE TAPPED A FINGER on the parchment envelope beneath the folded hands of the woman seated across from her. "Now that you've drawn it out of the box, you have to read it, Miss Emmy Lou."

"I never should have taken it," Miss Emmy Lou said. "I'm too old for this."

Molly leaned forward. "My grandmother always said, 'The day you're too old for dreams, you're ready to push up daisies.'"

"Happy thought," Miss Emmy Lou said. "But you're probably right. It's just that—"

"You're nervous about what you'll find," Reese finished for her.

Miss Emmy Lou nodded. "Scared to death."

"You should have seen me earlier today," Molly said. "My hands were shaking."

"And Reese had to practically dare me to open mine," Brie said. Sitting at the table and talking about Hattie's fantasies had eased some of her tension. At least it had gotten her mind off of Cody.

But even as the thought occurred to her, she slid her gaze to where he stood near the stage. He'd be there, she told herself, her guardian angel, when Avery finally introduced her.

"Taking out that parchment was the best thing I ever did," Reese said.

"Ditto." Brie and Molly spoke at the same time.

Reese narrowed her eyes on them. "You two act pretty fast."

"Once I saw what was on my parchment, I realized I'd wasted way too much time," Molly said. She slipped it out of her pocket and read aloud: "'You will recapture all of the sensuous delights you discovered with your first love.' After I read it, I knew that's exactly what I wanted. That's been my fantasy ever since I returned to the island."

"You're still in love with Nate," Reese said. "I thought the fantasy was supposed to get you beyond that."

"That was the plan," Molly admitted. "But when I read it this afternoon, something shifted in my mind. It started me thinking. When I was seventeen, my big dream was to go to fashion school in New York. Then Nate and I started dating and I knew that he was the one. I'm not sure I can explain it—but it's a feeling you get right in your gut. And you know."

"Yeah," Reese agreed with a smile.

Brie only managed a nod. The fact that she knew exactly what Molly was talking about sent her stomach into freefall. Cody couldn't be the one for her. He was her onetime fling.

"The thing is—if Nate hadn't dumped me, I would have stayed here," Molly continued. "I never would have left him to go to New York. So, I had a talk with him this afternoon."

"Just a talk?" Reese asked.

"Yeah." She made a little face. "He's working on

something. But I asked him, point blank, if he dumped me on purpose so that I'd go to fashion school. And he admitted that he had. As it turns out, he still has some crazy idea that I only came back here because my grandmother got ill. He thinks I still want to go back to New York."

"What did you do then?" Brie asked.

Molly smiled slowly. "I set him straight on that. And—" she turned her palm over to reveal a key card "—I'm going to meet him in his room later to finish our discussion. Only we're going to do a lot more than talk."

Reese clapped her hands together, and Brie found herself joining in the applause.

Then Molly turned to Miss Emmy Lou. "Your turn."

"You don't have to tell anyone what it is," Reese reminded her.

Brie noted that before she opened the envelope, Miss Emmy Lou's gaze shifted, too—all the way to the back of the bar. The instant the older woman turned her attention to the envelope, Brie risked a glance over her shoulder. A tall man with distinguished-looking gray hair stood near the door. He reminded her a bit of Paul Newman. By the time she looked back at Miss Emmy Lou, the woman was frowning at the opened paper.

"Don't worry if it doesn't seem to fit," Reese said. "Hattie works in mysterious ways."

"I'm supposed to discover all the joys of being with a younger man." Miss Emmy Lou blushed. "At my age."

"I checked Colonel Jenkins out online last month after he asked you to have coffee with him," Molly said. "He's only eight years younger than you are."

Brie glanced over her shoulder again. "We're talking about the Paul Newman look-alike standing near the back door, right?"

"Correct," Reese said. "He's also the son of Hattie's lover. And Samuel Jenkins the first was at least ten years younger than Hattie."

"That was then," Miss Emmy Lou said.

"And this is now," Brie said. "Age isn't such a big deal anymore. Look at Demi Moore and that Ashton whatever his name is." Out of the corner of her eye, she could see Avery approaching. Her cue was coming up, and she never missed one.

"My advice to you, Miss Emmy Lou, is to grab him. He's a hottie." Then, drawing in a deep breath, Brie looked at Reese. "Has anyone ever drawn a second fantasy out of the box?"

"Not that I know of."

Brie turned to Avery. "I'd like another crack at the box after I sing."

"Fine with me." He gave her his megawatt smile as he led her toward the stage.

As he introduced her, Brie's eyes collided again with Cody's. Yeah. She had a different fantasy in mind entirely for Cody Marsh. And the first chance she got, she was going to let him know.

CODY KEPT BRIE IN HIS peripheral vision as Avery drew her onto the small stage and lifted her onto the piano. "Ladies and gentlemen," Avery said. "We have a special treat tonight. New York City lounge singer Brie Sullivan has agreed to perform for us."

There was a smattering of applause. The bass player and the saxophonist joined Avery as he left the stage.

Conversation faded as the light from the overhead chandeliers dimmed.

Out of the corner of his eye, Cody was aware that Brie crossed her legs and leaned back against her hands. Chanteuse position. He might have smiled, but he kept his focus on the guests, scanning faces. Avery had begun his circuit around the U-shaped bar. He, too, watched the crowd.

Then she started singing. Without any accompaniment at first. Just her voice. Soft and dreamy, it slowly swelled until it filled the room and went straight to his gut. After a few bars, the piano came in beneath her.

It was an old song, "Someone to Watch Over Me." But he'd never heard it sung with such wistful sadness, such longing. It tugged at something deep inside of him.

And he wasn't the only one being pulled in. The room had gone quiet. Everyone within his view was watching Brie. Cody focused on the faces, knowing Nate, the colonel, Avery and Mac were doing the same.

When the last note hung on the air and then faded, the crowd burst into applause. Cody joined them, but he kept his gaze on the faces. The only expression that stood out was Mac Davies'. He looked surprised. Cody stiffened, but when he caught Mac's eye, the man shook his head.

Brie leaned over to say something to the pianist, then began a little patter with her audience. She was good.

Brie began her second song, a Sinatra classic, "Luck Be a Lady Tonight." It wasn't a bad selection for an audience that had gathered for a Singles Weekend featuring a fantasy box. But it would have been an even better choice for that Las Vegas gig she'd missed out on.

It occurred to him that luck was just what he needed. And just what Brie needed, too.

She started the second chorus, and that was when it hit him. He knew exactly what had been nagging at him all day. Radtke and partner had needed more than luck if their accident plan on the hillside had any hope of succeeding. They would have needed some prior knowledge of the road that led from Belle Bay to Haworth House.

He'd been so sure that no one could have known that he would bring Brie to Haworth House. But obviously, he'd been wrong.

And they needed to be looking for that person as well as Radtke's partner.

He moved toward Nate and told him what he was thinking.

He'd made his way to Mac to ask him to pass the information on to Avery and the colonel when Brie segued into a new song. This one told the story of lovers struggling to find a time and a place to be together.

The instant his gaze locked with hers, he couldn't look away. She was singing to him, pouring all the haunting tragedy, all the longing in the music and the lyrics right into him. For a moment, he was completely seduced—right out of the moment. It was as if they were totally alone in the room.

"Somewhere." As the word filled the air, she held him and the audience captive in the emotion.

He couldn't look away. And if he hadn't been looking at her, hadn't been totally entranced, he would have missed seeing the figure materialize beside her on the piano. Hattie.

Then the lights went out.

"Get down!" He shouted the words, praying Brie already had as a gunshot shattered the mirror behind her.

# 10

ANOTHER SHOT RANG OUT.

Brie could feel the heat as it whipped past her.

People screamed. More mirror shards rained down.

"Everybody get down!"

Brie already had. She'd flattened herself on the top of the piano and started wiggling her way across its surface the instant she'd felt that other presence beside her.

A third shot rang out. She heard a bullet thump into the Steinway just before she slithered off the piano and dropped to the floor of the stage. Her knees absorbed the brunt of the impact. Then strong hands grabbed her waist, and someone flattened her to the floor in the narrow space behind the stage.

Cody. Her body recognized his even before he breathed in her ear, "Are you all right? Did that shot get you?"

"No," she whispered back. "I'm fine."

The room had fallen into an eerie silence. She could hear Cody's breath as she struggled to get her own back. At least no shots were being fired.

A loud grunt followed by a crash came from the back of the bar.

"We've got him," a male voice said. Brie thought it was Mac's.

There were gasps and questions from the spectators.

"What's going on?"

"Were those gun shots?"

"Stay where you are. We're getting the lights on."

Brie recognized Avery's voice. Then Cody whispered in her ear, "Stay here. I want them to believe they got you."

"They? I thought they got—"

"There may be two." Cody levered himself off of her, crouched for a second to peer over the top of the stage. Then he was gone.

Fear slammed into her, icing her veins. Someone was still out there with a gun. And Cody had gone after that person, too? She tried to count the passing seconds, but everything in her system had slowed—heart, brain, lungs.

When she finally drew in a breath, the pain in her chest told her just how much she'd needed the air. Suddenly, she had to know. Moving as quietly as she could, she got to her hands and knees and then peered over the top of the stage as Cody had done.

Avery was talking in a calm voice. "Just a few moments longer. We're working on the lights."

The room wasn't as pitch black as it had seemed at first. The electricity was out, but the dim glow of candles on the tables offered some light.

Whoever had gotten off those shots would be able to tell that she wasn't sitting on the piano anymore.

Would they be fooled into thinking their mission was accomplished?

And where was Cody?

Brie saw a shadow separate itself from others at the bar and move in the direction of the lobby. Then there was a blur of movement as another figure flew at the first. They went down and rolled. The struggle was brief.

A flashlight snapped on, but it only illuminated a small area. Beyond the piano legs, Brie could just make out that Cody was straddling a still body. Nate stood nearby, his gun drawn.

"What have we here?" Nate asked.

Cody reached down and pulled a wig off the body beneath his. "Meet Federal Marshal Maxine Norville."

THREE HOURS LATER CODY leaned against the bar, listening to a progress report from Nate on his cell phone. Avery and Mac were seated next to him on stools. But he had a better view of Brie if he stood. And he wasn't ready to let her out of his sight yet.

She'd come through the evening with nothing more than a scraped knee. It could have been worse.

Shifting his glance only slightly to the right, he could see the bullet that had entered the Steinway. But it was the first shot, the one that had shattered the mirror that would have gotten her if he hadn't seen Hattie materialize.

If he hadn't been looking at Brie, hadn't been so entranced by her and the song, he might have missed Hattie, and he wouldn't have shouted out the warning in time.

He hadn't a doubt in the world that Hattie had been

watching out for Brie, that she'd appeared on that piano
to send him a signal.

"You still there?" Nate said into his ear.

"Yeah." He was here and so was Brie. That was what
he had to focus on.

She and Reese were enjoying a well-deserved brandy
in a nearby booth. Colonel Jenkins and Miss Emmy
Lou Pritchard had drifted off to a separate table at the
back of the bar very close to where the colonel and Mac
had brought down the man they believed worked with
Radtke. The earlier crowd had thinned, but the extra
excitement the evening had provided hadn't scared all
of them off.

Molly had followed Nate earlier when he and his
deputy escorted his two prisoners down to Belle Bay's
jail.

"Radtke's partner is cooperating," Nate said.

"So soon?"

"Well, I pointed out to him that he was caught with
night vision goggles and a recently fired gun. And since
he hadn't killed anyone, I hinted that his cooperation
might get him a deal. He admitted to installing an elec-
tronic device that allowed him to turn off the power
in the hotel by remote control. That's all I got out of
him before the Feds and the U.S. Marshals invaded my
office. Molly, Tim and I are confined to the space immediately surrounding my desk."

"That bad, huh?"

"Luckily, they're all on their cell phones. That's how
I can keep track of the progress they're making. They
don't have much use for us locals."

"Their mistake," Cody said.

"The good news is that Maxine Norville wants a deal.
If they give her one and put her in witness protection,

she'll tell all. Seems she's been working for the Ferrante family for some time, and they turned on the pressure when the first hit on Brie failed. Maxine claims that it was fear for her life that forced her to become more actively involved."

"And since she didn't want anyone looking at her as the source of the leak in the marshal's office, she handed Brie over to me," Cody murmured, "and then called some pros in to get rid of both of us in one fell swoop."

"You must have read her mind," Nate commented. After a slight pause, he continued, "You know, we might have had a much different ending here if you hadn't figured out Maxine Norville was in on the hit."

"Yeah." Cody didn't like dwelling on that. "We can thank Brie for that. If she hadn't sung that song, I might never have figured out that Radtke and her buddy had needed more than luck to set up the 'accident.' I should have put it together earlier. I just couldn't figure out how anyone could have known I'd bring Brie to Haworth House. Once I accepted that Radtke or her partner had to have had some previous knowledge of that hill, then I knew Maxine was in on it. I'm betting she bugged my apartment before she called me in on the case. It was only a matter of minutes after I talked to her that I called Avery to make the reservation. After she learned that, all she had to do was pass the information on to Radtke and pal."

Cody heard a voice in the background.

"I've got to go," Nate said. "Pass on the news to the others. Molly and I'll probably be here all night. I'll keep you updated."

As soon as he pocketed his cell, Cody filled Mac and Avery in.

Avery raised his beer. "All's well that ends well."

Cody switched his gaze back to Reese and Brie. The problem was that he didn't want what he was discovering with Brie to end.

When Avery hurried over to pass the news on to the two women, Mac turned to Cody. "It's not the end yet for Brie, is it? She'll still have to testify against Ferrante on Monday?"

"That's the plan," Cody said. And that was part of his problem. She still had to get through the trial. And there was still a good chance she might have to go back into witness protection. "But now that Maxine's in custody and the marshal's office is under scrutiny, she'll be safe. At any rate, I won't be leaving her side."

Mac glanced at Brie and then back at Cody. "What do you know about Brie's background?"

Cody's brows shot up. "What's your interest?"

"When I first heard her sing…for a moment, I was certain I'd heard her voice before. Is she by any chance adopted?"

"Yes. When she was two," Cody said. "I checked, but the records are sealed."

Mac nodded. "I know I've never seen her perform before tonight. I wouldn't have forgotten."

"I doubt anyone would," Avery added as he rejoined them. "A set of pipes like that doesn't come along very often. I heard Streisand live once when I was a kid. Brie made me think of her."

Mac shook his head. "It wasn't Streisand that she reminded me of. But I'm almost sure I've heard that voice before. It'll come back to me. In the meantime, I think I'm going to collect Reese. It's been a long day for her." He glanced at Avery. "For all of us."

Cody's cell phone rang.

"More good news," Nate said on the other end. "One of the Feds here just got a call. Dicky Ferrante will not be going to trial on Monday or any other day. He's making a deal with the Feds as well, and he's singing his lungs out. So we've got a competition going on between Dicky and Maxine to see who can tell the most and work out the better deal."

"News certainly travels fast."

Nate laughed on the other end of the phone. "All it takes is a dozen or so men in suits, all on their cells." Then he cut the connection.

Cody repocketed his phone and signaled Avery and Mac to follow him to the booth where he passed on Nate's good news.

"So I'm a free woman?" Brie asked. "I can go back to my old life?"

"Perhaps an even better one," Mac said. "I can put you in contact with people in the music business out in L.A."

Reese reached across the table and took her hand. "And you could probably use a new agent. I'm going to call mine first thing in the morning."

Brie pressed her free hand to her heart. "Oh, my God. I don't think I can breathe. I—"

"I'll get the champagne," Avery said.

"And the fantasy box," Brie said. "You promised me I could draw out a new one."

"That I did," Avery said.

Cody's stomach sank. And something clutched tight around his heart when Avery brought over the box. Why in hell did she want a new fantasy?

Only one answer occurred to him. She was ready to move on. He watched her dig deep for an envelope.

But when she drew it out, she didn't open it. Instead, she handed it to him. "I don't want to read it until we're in the tower room. Coming?"

BY THE TIME THEY'D CLIMBED the iron stairs, Brie wasn't sure she'd be able to speak. She had the speech planned. She'd even practiced it with Reese while they'd been sipping brandy. But this was where she wanted to deliver it.

Hattie had helped her before. In those few seconds before the mirror had shattered behind her, she'd known that she'd sensed another presence on that piano. Not that she'd seen anything. But she was almost sure she'd had help dodging that bullet.

Now she needed Hattie's help again. And she'd taken precautions to have it. That's why she'd asked Avery to let her draw out another fantasy. Because she didn't want the onetime fling. She wanted more.

The problem was that sometimes, you just couldn't have more. She was getting her old life back and then some. Mac Davies and Reese were going to open doors for her that never would have been opened before. Twenty-four hours ago, that would have been enough. But not now. She still wanted more.

Brie walked into the darkened room on legs she couldn't feel. Moonlight poured through the windows, leaving rectangular patterns on the floor. The sound of her footsteps echoed eerily.

She couldn't remember when she'd ever been this nervous, this scared. Not when Avery had lifted her onto the piano earlier and she'd known there was a killer in the room. Not hiding behind that same piano, dodging bullets—and not even that morning when the motorcycle had nearly forced them off the road.

*That morning.* Yesterday, she hadn't known Cody. How could he have been in her life such a short amount of time and still have become so…essential?

There was a click, and a soft light filled the room. It was only then that she caught a glimpse of herself in the beveled mirror. The other image in the glass faded instantly. But not before she recognized the woman who'd sung to her from the Steinway.

And the melody filled her mind. "When You Wish Upon a Star." Drawing in a deep breath, she shifted her gaze to one of the windows. There were thousands of stars out there, but all she needed was one. The brightest one. Then, closing her eyes, she made the wish and prayed with all her heart that it would come true.

"Why did you take another fantasy, Brie?"

Pressing her hand against her stomach, she turned to face Cody. "I decided I didn't want the old one."

"But you do want a new one." That was the fear that had been pounding through him ever since they'd left the bar. From what he'd learned about Hattie's fantasies, they were designed to hook you up with one person—for good.

"That's right."

Brie wanted someone new. Cody felt as if someone had opened up his chest, closed hard hands around his heart and squeezed.

"So you've decided to move on."

"Yes."

"No." When he lifted the parchment envelope she'd given to him, he discovered that he'd already crushed it. No matter. After smoothing it out, he ripped it in two and tossed it on the floor.

Brie took a quick step back. "What did you—"

"You're not going to have a new fantasy," he said as

he started toward her. As he passed the computer desk, he picked up the parchment envelope he'd dropped there earlier. "And you're sure you don't want the old one?"

"I'm sure." But she wasn't meeting his eyes. She was staring at his hands.

"Good. I was never a fan of onetime flings."

She met his eyes then. "You read my fantasy?"

He raised his brows. "You left it lying around. I'm a trained investigator." Then he ripped the envelope in half.

"No."

She took a quick step toward it and was about to lean down when Cody grabbed her wrists. "I'm not letting you move on, Brie. Not without me. If you want new fantasies, they're going to be with me, too."

Her head went into a spin and she couldn't seem to pull air into her lungs again. She was going to have to work on that. A singer needed to breathe. And maybe, just maybe, she hadn't heard him correctly. At any rate, she needed to know. Using all her strength, she drew in a breath and tried to clear her mind. "And what if I don't want new fantasies?"

"What do you want?" he asked.

She could see what was in his eyes now. A trace of anger, a glint of fear. But there was more. And it was the more that gave her the courage to speak. "I want you. I have from the first moment I saw you. I don't understand it."

He smiled slowly. "Looks like we're on even ground then. I wanted you in that same instant. I want you now. For keeps."

"For keeps." She just had time to get the words out before he closed his mouth over hers and dragged her to the floor.

His hands made quick work of her dress, his whisper hot in her ear. "I've wanted you out of that since you put it on."

Heat exploded then. She heard the slide of silk as he shot it across the floor, then the snap of his jeans, the scratch of a zipper. As he rose above her, thrust into her, Brie was sure that lightning crackled in the room.

His eyes were so dark. She found his hands and linked her fingers with his as he rocked into her. "It's not a onetime fling if we do this again. And again."

"No." Pleasure rippled through her, filling all the empty spaces. But when she would have arched against him, he held her still. "You want your career, and you'll have it. You're amazing."

"I thought it was all I wanted. All I could have."

"Yeah." He smiled down at her. "But now we can have more."

Something inside of her melted and flowed into him.

"I'll show you," he said.

And he did.

A long time later, they lay on the floor in front of the mirror. Her head was on his shoulder, his arms holding her tight.

"I'm surprised that lightning didn't strike us both when you started ripping up those fantasies."

He turned his head and grinned at her. "In a way, it did."

She grinned right back. "True."

"But I've been thinking about your fantasy ever since I read it. And I have a theory."

"Don't keep me in suspense."

"I'm thinking that a onetime fling may have been the fantasy that originally brought Hattie and Samuel together. He was younger, married and had a child. The Brightmans found out that the two of them originally met at the library. And maybe it happened for them, the same way it happened for us. Just like that."

"And the onetime fling fantasy was so tempting. They couldn't resist it," Brie said.

"Exactly. But once they'd made love, they couldn't resist the temptation of doing it again."

"And again," Brie said as she rolled on top of him.

He lifted her hips, entered her. "For keeps, Brie."

They began to move then, slowly. Until they became so lost in each other that they didn't see how the mirror behind them glowed.

# *Epilogue*

AVERY TAPPED A SPOON against a glass to get the attention of the small group that had gathered in the bar. Singles Weekend outdoor activities were in full swing, leaving the hotel relatively quiet.

"I want to propose a toast," Avery said. "To Hattie's fantasy box." He raised his glass of champagne. The old-fashioned linen covered hat box sat in a prominent place on the bar. Everyone joined in the toast.

"May the fantasies live on," Cody added. But it was Brie's eyes he met before he drank. Out of the corner of his eye, he noted that the other men who sat at the bar—Dane and Ian MacFarland and Mac Davies—also toasted their respective women. The MacFarland brothers, along with Naomi and Jillian, had reached Haworth House earlier in the day.

"For a lifetime," Reese added.

"And beyond," Brie added.

"Good point," Jillian said. "I believe that Hattie and Samuel are still enjoying their fantasies."

"May we all be as lucky as they are," Naomi said.

Everyone raised their glasses again.

Brie sat with the Brightman sisters in a nearby booth. Naomi and Jillian were determined to get all the first-hand details of the adventures from Reese and Brie. Cody assumed that the MacFarland brothers had invited Mac and him to join them at the bar for the same reason. Cody hadn't had a chance to talk to Ian yet, though he soon would. He knew his friend was a stickler for details.

To postpone the interrogation, he turned to the men and lifted his glass again. "I want to propose a toast to Avery Cooper. Long may he be the keeper of the hat box."

"I'll second that." Mac turned to Avery. "If you hadn't come up with the idea of this Singles Weekend, I might never have met Reese. I'd put a lot of effort into avoiding that. And I'd purposely scheduled my visit here at a time when she was supposed to be in L.A."

"I owe Ian for my first visit to Haworth House," Cody said. "If I hadn't seen Samuel and felt almost compelled to return, I might never have brought Brie here. And if it weren't for the Singles Weekend, she might never have drawn out her fantasy."

Avery patted the top of the hat box. "Hattie works in mysterious ways."

"Not to take any credit away from Hattie, but I think we also should toast Avery for the job he's done getting this room back into shape," Dane said. "Of course, I got my information third-hand through Naomi from Reese, but I don't see much evidence that the big shoot-out Ian and I missed even occurred."

Dane was right. Somehow Avery had managed to get the place cleaned and the mirrors replaced—on a

Saturday morning. The bar at Haworth House would be ready to open for business at five o'clock that evening.

"There's just the bullet hole in the Steinway," Mac said. "But I checked it out last night. The damage is cosmetic. A talented carpenter can repair it, and the piano still plays in perfect tune. I tried it out."

"You play the piano?" Cody asked.

Mac shrugged. "My adoptive parents had money, enough to afford ten years of piano lessons. They wanted me to be well-rounded."

Cody turned to Ian and Dane. "I figure you have to have some questions other than how Avery was able to get the bar back in running order."

Ian looked at Dane. "We don't have any questions at the moment."

"I paid Nate a visit shortly after I arrived," Dane explained. "He wasn't happy to be disturbed, but he gave me all the information he has to date." He turned to Mac and added, "Chantal Dutoit's attorney is trying to work out a plea with the D.A. The L.A. police are also interested in talking to her. Interested enough to send someone here to the hospital on the mainland where she's being held. It seems she may have tried to help her brother out on other occasions. They want to talk to Charles, too."

Ian turned to Cody. "The only update Nate had on the Maxine Norville case was that the suits have left his office. Dane and I have a contact in New York City who'll keep his ear to the ground. But Brie's definitely clear of the whole mess."

"That's excellent news," Cody said. "But I thought for sure Avery called us together for a debriefing."

Avery shrugged. "It was Mac and Reese who asked me to call everyone together."

"My idea really," Mac said. "I wanted a chance to hear Brie sing again. I have a theory I wanted to test out. It's a bit of a wild one. But the more I think about it, the more right it feels. So I talked it over with Reese, and she said we should make it a family gathering."

Family? He and Brie weren't strictly family. Cody glanced over to see Reese sliding out of the booth, and the other women followed. As they reached the bar, each one of them joined their man.

With Reese at his side, Mac turned to Brie. "When you sang last night, I was sure I'd heard your voice before. I just couldn't place it. I'm hoping if you sing for me again, I'll figure it out."

"Sure," Brie said. "Anything special you want me to try?"

"Yes, there is," Mac said as he led her to the piano and lifted her on top of it. Then he sat at the keyboard and ran his fingers over the keys. "I want you to sing the song you heard Hattie singing—'When You Wish Upon a Star.'"

"Got it," Brie said. She waited for Mac to play a little introduction before she came in.

No one said a word as Brie's voice filled the room. There was a wistfulness, a longing in the sound that tightened something around Cody's heart. And he wasn't the only one who was affected. He was sitting close enough to Ian to note when his friend gripped Dane's arm. And what he glimpsed on the two brothers' faces mimicked what he'd seen on Mac's face when he'd first heard Brie the night before. A mix of surprise and... recognition?

Ian leaned over to whisper something to his brother, but Cody couldn't catch it because at that moment, he was sure he heard another voice blend with Brie's. His attention shifted immediately to the piano. For just an instant, he saw Hattie sitting next to Brie in chanteuse position.

Then the last note died away, and Brie was once more alone. Everyone applauded. But Mac moved first, rising from the piano bench to take Brie's hands in his.

When Ian and Dane slid off their stools to move to the edge of the stage, Cody followed. So did the others.

"I talked with Reese," Mac said glancing down at Ian and Dane. "But I didn't want to say anything to you until I was sure. Now I am." Then he turned to Brie. "Your voice reminds me of my mother's. I remember her singing that song all the time. Cody says you're adopted. I'm wondering if you might be my sister."

"Your sister?" Brie asked.

"I was four when my mom died and our family split up," Mac continued. "But I do remember that I had a little sister and two older brothers." He turned to face Ian and Dane. "Reese told me that you were both separated from your family, too. And if I can trust my four-year-old self's memory, my brothers' names were Ian and Dane. Everything here has happened so fast. I didn't put the possibilities together until Reese and I had a chance to talk last night—after all the excitement."

Reese turned to Ian and Dane. "Mac wanted to hear Brie sing again, just to be sure. Is there a way you two can find out for sure if the four of you are related?"

Dane spoke first. "Our little sister's name was Briana."

"Our little brother's name was Caleb," Ian said.

"That was my name," Mac said. "My parents chose to call me Mac. I always thought it was my middle name. I called them this morning to check for sure. They said

Mac is short for MacFarland, which was my last name when they adopted me."

Dane held out his hand to Mac. "Now that we know who your adoptive parents are, Ian can probably access those records."

"And I have a good chance of getting access to Briana MacFarland's adoption records when I go to court tomorrow afternoon," Naomi said.

"But I don't think we'll need them. Dane and I remember the voice, too. And the song. You sound just like her." Ian climbed onto the stage and drew Brie into his arms for a hug. "Hi, sis."

For a few moments, Brie was caught up in a round of hugs and questions. The moment he saw the tears blur her eyes, Cody went to her and drew her close. "Take a deep breath."

"I know. I keep forgetting to do that." Once she did, she met his eyes. "I've always had these dreams about having three big brothers. I thought it was a fantasy, but it's real. Then you were my fantasy. And you're real, too."

"You can count on it. For keeps."

Behind them, the three MacFarland brothers had moved to the piano again. Mac was playing. All three of them were singing about wishing on a star.

"I should join them," Brie said.

"We all should." As Cody led her to the piano, he glanced back at Avery.

The man was still at the bar. He grinned at Cody as he gave the fantasy box another approving pat.

And Cody was almost sure he could hear Hattie's voice and another deeper one join in the song.

* * * * *

HARLEQUIN *Blaze*

# COMING NEXT MONTH

## Available August 31, 2010

HBCNM0810

# REQUEST YOUR FREE BOOKS!

## 2 FREE NOVELS
## PLUS 2
## FREE GIFTS!

♦ HARLEQUIN®

*Blaze*

**Red-hot reads!**

**YES!** Please send me 2 FREE Harlequin® Blaze™ novels and my 2 FREE gifts (gifts are worth about $10). After receiving them, if I don't wish to receive any more books, I can return the shipping statement marked "cancel." If I don't cancel, I will receive 6 brand-new novels every month and be billed just $4.24 per book in the U.S. or $4.71 per book in Canada. That's a saving of at least 15% off the cover price. It's quite a bargain. Shipping and handling is just 50¢ per book.* I understand that accepting the 2 free books and gifts places me under no obligation to buy anything. I can always return a shipment and cancel at any time. Even if I never buy another book, the two free books and gifts are mine to keep forever.

151/351 HDN E5LS

Name _____ (PLEASE PRINT)

Address _____ Apt. #

City _____ State/Prov. _____ Zip/Postal Code

Signature (if under 18, a parent or guardian must sign)

### Mail to the Harlequin Reader Service:
**IN U.S.A.:** P.O. Box 1867, Buffalo, NY 14240-1867
**IN CANADA:** P.O. Box 609, Fort Erie, Ontario L2A 5X3

Not valid for current subscribers to Harlequin Blaze books.

**Want to try two free books from another line?**
**Call 1-800-873-8635 or visit www.morefreebooks.com.**

* Terms and prices subject to change without notice. Prices do not include applicable taxes. N.Y. residents add applicable sales tax. Canadian residents will be charged applicable provincial taxes and GST. Offer not valid in Quebec. This offer is limited to one order per household. All orders subject to approval. Credit or debit balances in a customer's account(s) may be offset by any other outstanding balance owed by or to the customer. Please allow 4 to 6 weeks for delivery. Offer available while quantities last.

**Your Privacy:** Harlequin Books is committed to protecting your privacy. Our Privacy Policy is available online at www.eHarlequin.com or upon request from the Reader Service. From time to time we make our lists of customers available to reputable third parties who may have a product or service of interest to you. If you would prefer we not share your name and address, please check here. ☐

**Help us get it right**—We strive for accurate, respectful and relevant communications. To clarify or modify your communication preferences, visit us at www.ReaderService.com/consumerschoice.

HB10R

# HARLEQUIN®

## A *Romance*

### FOR EVERY MOOD™

Spotlight on
## — Heart & Home —

Heartwarming romances
where love can happen
right when you least expect it.

See the next page to enjoy a sneak peek
from Harlequin Superromance®,
a Heart and Home series.

*Enjoy a sneak peek at fan favorite Molly O'Keefe's
Harlequin Superromance miniseries,*
THE NOTORIOUS O'NEILLS, *with*
*TYLER O'NEILL'S REDEMPTION,*
*available September 2010
only from Harlequin Superromance.*

Police chief Juliette Tremblant recognized the shape of the man strolling down the street—in as calm and leisurely fashion as if it were the middle of the day rather than midnight. She slowed her car, convinced her eyes were playing tricks on her. It had been a long time since Tyler O'Neill had been seen in this town.

As she pulled to a stop at the curb, he turned toward her, and her heart about stopped.

"What the hell are you doing here, Tyler?"

"Well, if it isn't Juliette Tremblant." He made his way over to her, then leaned down so he could look her in the eye. He was close enough to touch.

Juliette was not, repeat, *not* going to touch Tyler O'Neill. Not with her fingers. Not with a ten-foot pole. There would be no touching. Which was too bad, since it was the only way she was ever going to convince herself the man standing in front of her—as rumpled and heart-stoppingly handsome now as he'd been at sixteen—was real.

And not a figment of all her furious revenge dreams.

"What are you doing back in Bonne Terre?" she asked.

"The manor is sitting empty," Tyler said and shrugged, as though his arriving out of the blue after ten years was casual. "Seems like someone should be watching over the family home."

"You?" She laughed at the very notion of him being here for any unselfish reason. "Please."

He stared at her for a second, then smiled. Her heart fluttered against her chest—a small mechanical bird powered by that smile.

"You're right." But that cryptic comment was all he offered.

Juliette bit her lip against the other questions.

*Why did you go?*

*Why didn't you write? Call?*

*What did I do?*

But what would be the point? Ten years of silence were all the answer she really needed.

She had sworn off feeling anything for this man long ago. Yet one look at him and all the old hurt and rage resurfaced as though they'd been waiting for the chance. That made her mad.

She put the car in gear, determined not to waste another minute thinking about Tyler O'Neill. "Have a good night, Tyler," she said, liking all the cool "go screw yourself" she managed to fit into those words.

*It seems Juliette has an old score to settle with Tyler.*
*Pick up TYLER O'NEILL'S REDEMPTION*
*to see how he makes it up to her.*
*Available September 2010,*
*only from Harlequin Superromance.*

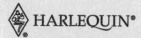
HARLEQUIN®

*American* ★ *Romance*®

# TANYA MICHAELS
## Texas Baby

Babies
&
Bachelors
USA

Instant parenthood is turning Addie Caine's life
upside down. Caring for her young nephew and
infant niece is rewarding—but exhausting! So when
a gorgeous man named Giff Baker starts a short-term
assignment at her office, Addie knows there's no time
for romance. Yet Giff seems to be in hot pursuit....
Is this part of his job, or can he really be falling
for her? And her chaotic, ready-made family!

**Available September 2010
wherever books are sold.**

**"LOVE, HOME & HAPPINESS"**

# MARGARET WAY

### *introduces*

## The lives & loves of
## Australia's most powerful family

Growing up in the spotlight hasn't been easy, but the two
Rylance heirs, Corin and his sister, Zara, have come of age
and are ready to claim their inheritance. Though they are
privileged, proud and powerful, they are about to discover
that there are some things money can't buy....

### *Look for:*

# *Australia's Most Eligible Bachelor*
#### *Available September*

# *Cattle Baron Needs a Bride*
#### *Available October*